TWO GUNS TO AVALON

Center Point
Large Print

Also by Barry Cord and available from Center Point Large Print:

Sheriff of Big Hat

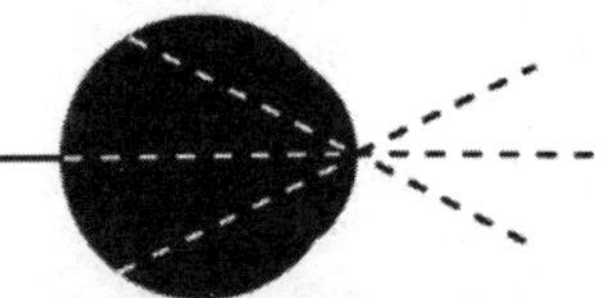

TWO GUNS TO AVALON

Barry Cord

CENTER POINT LARGE PRINT
THORNDIKE, MAINE

This Center Point Large Print edition
is published in the year 2017 by arrangement with
Golden West Literary Agency.

First US edition: Arcadia House
First UK edition: Hale

The text of this Large Print edition is unabridged.
In other aspects, this book may vary
from the original edition.
Printed in the United States of America
on permanent paper.
Set in 16-point Times New Roman type.

ISBN: 978-1-68324-591-9 (hardcover)
ISBN: 978-1-68324-595-7 (paperback)

Library of Congress Cataloging-in-Publication Data

Names: Cord, Barry, 1913-1983, author.
Title: Two guns to avalon / Barry Cord.
Description: Center Point large print edition. | Thorndike, Maine :
Center Point Large Print, 2017.
Identifiers: LCCN 2017039220| ISBN 9781683245919
(hardcover : alk. paper) | ISBN 9781683245957 (pbk. : alk. paper)
Subjects: LCSH: Large type books. | GSAFD: Western stories.
Classification: LCC PS3505.O6646 T89 2017 | DDC 813/.54—dc23
LC record available at https://lccn.loc.gov/2017039220

TWO GUNS TO AVALON

CHAPTER ONE

— The Devil Rides Armed —

They were still bringing in the dead and injured from the Santa Fe train wreck eleven miles out of town when Ben Craig pulled up before the sheriff's office. Boxwood City was a mining town not too far from the county line, and the sheriff, surly from a night's fruitless riding at the head of a hastily assembled posse, met Ben at the door.

Ben took out his wallet and showed him his identification, and Sheriff Johnson growled: "Wells Fargo man, eh?"

Ben said evenly: "Ben Craig, special agent."

Johnson's tired gaze held on Ben with flash of interest. "Heard of you," he said, unsmiling. "Always wanted to see what you were like." His smile was cold. "From some of the stories, I was looking for a man nine feet tall."

He waved Ben to a chair, closed the door and stood looking at Craig, a tired man, not pleased with himself.

"See the wreck?"

Ben nodded. "Rode by on my way in. There was a wrecking crew pulling up to a flat car, but it didn't seem to me there was much they could salvage of the engine."

Johnson shrugged. "Dynamite blew it clean off the rails! Killed the engineer and fireman." He walked slowly back to the desk, plucked a cigar from a box and eyed it morosely for a moment before putting it between his lips. He looked at Ben. "The baggage man was killed by the Sonora Kid or his partner—"

"Partner?" Ben's voice held surprise.

Johnson nodded curtly. "Had a man with him this time." He smiled a tired smile. "Guess the Kid figgered a ninety-thousand-dollar haul rated one."

Ben stood a moment, turning his gaze to an old poster tacked on the sheriff's bulletin board. Posters like it were in every Wells Fargo office.

$10,000 REWARD
for
THE SONORA KID
Dead or Alive.

There was no description of the Kid . . . no picture. Few people had seen him; none could identify him. But he usually headed South across the Mexican Border after a holdup, which accounted for the name of the "Sonora Kid." He was, it was generally agreed, a very dangerous man.

The sheriff broke in on Ben, his voice surly. "The conductor swears the Kid's companion was wounded; said he saw him slump over as they rode off. But he was still riding a fast trail when we turned back at the county line!"

Ben turned to look at Johnson. At twenty-nine Ben still had the hard drive of youth, tempered by the cautious hand of experience. A slim man, six feet, with a wiry toughness, he had worked in the Pinkerton Denver Office before becoming a Wells Fargo special agent.

Out in the street the carriages were rolling in, bringing to town the last of the injured. The sun was not yet an hour high, but the town had a midday bustle and excitement. Ben took a short breath.

"How much of a start do they have, Sheriff?"

"Six . . . seven hours." Johnson remembered the unlighted cigar in his mouth and scraped a match on his thumbnail. He was a big man, a little used by years of riding the thin line between justice and expediency . . . a square-faced man who had resigned himself to achieving less than he was capable of.

"My jurisdiction stops at the county line," he said. "But you don't have to worry about that, do you?"

Ben shook his head. "What kind of horses were they riding?"

"The Kid was riding a piebald. His companion

rode a gray horse." Johnson reached for his hat, hanging on a peg by the desk. "They'll be keepin' wide of towns on their way to the Mexican Border. With luck, you might head them off!"

The sheriff turned to the door. "Nothing more I can do. . . . I'm going to bed."

Ben joined him at the door; they went out. While the sheriff locked up, Ben crossed to his horse, a rangy buckskin, and mounted. He looked down a moment on Johnson, studying him. Finally: "Ten thousand dollars is a lot of reward money, Sheriff. Most men would forget county lines for a crack at it."

Johnson shook his head. "I'm not that good, Ben . . . on a horse, or with a gun! And," he smiled bitterly, "that ninety thousand dollars was Wells Fargo money, not mine!"

As Ben started to swing away from the rack, the sheriff added: "But like you say, that ten thousand dollars is a lot of money. Maybe you won't be the only one on the Kid's trail."

Ben stared at him with a narrow regard. "Who, Sheriff?"

Johnson shrugged. "Bounty hunter by the name of Sam Jelco. He met us at the county line, asked the same questions. . . ." He frowned at Ben's reaction. "You know Sam?"

Ben nodded. "I know him," he said coldly. He pulled his buckskin away from the rack and rode off down the street.

• • •

Two days later the Sonora Kid and his companion, Felipe, pulled up at the edge of a desert waterhole. The Kid slid stiffly from his saddle and turned to help his dying companion down. Felipe, his sun-blackened, stubbled face twisted with pain, made a gesture for the Kid to leave him.

"No more," he croaked. "No . . . more . . . ridin'. . . ."

The Kid, ignoring his request, turned to the waterhole. A high-riding sun glared up from the surface of the alkali-dusted water. He sank to his stomach, clearing the water with his right hand, and buried his hot, sun-blackened face into it. He let it soak through his dry skin, his cracked lips. He drank sparingly.

His piebald and the gray drank thirstily, standing fetlock deep in the shallow pool. The Kid turned back to Felipe, stiffening as he saw the gun in Felipe's hand.

"Felipe!" The Kid's cry tore harshly at his throat.

"Go . . . faster . . . without me!" Felipe whispered. He cocked the gun and shoved the muzzle under his chin. The Kid lunged for him, but Felipe pulled the trigger before the Kid could reach him.

The Kid turned away, his face graying. He stood looking off across the shimmering desert for a long moment. Then he turned back to the pool, glancing bitterly at his image before grabbing the reins of his piebald.

He was a slim, muscular man, between twenty and thirty years old. He had a fine-boned, sensitive face, and his dark brown eyes, red-rimmed from lack of sleep, carried the hot flame of idealism in their depths. He was dressed in old, nondescript range clothes, faded black pants tucked into run-over half boots. A red cotton handkerchief was knotted loosely at his throat.

He was armed with a single Navy Colt in a scuffed leather holster. A late model Winchester carbine jutted from the piebald's saddle scabbard.

He didn't look like much, standing there beside his tired piebald. He looked tired and hurt, shocked by the death of his friend. But time was pressing, and Felipe would have died before they crossed the desert. He had merely cut short the agony.

The Kid sucked in a deep breath, patting the bulging saddlebag. Ninety thousand dollars had come high, but it was worth it!

He lifted himself into saddle in a quick heave and forced the piebald's head out of the waterhole. Unwillingly he glanced at his back trail. Behind him lay almost a hundred miles of desert: a vast and empty desolation, avoided by all sane men. The Kid had taken that way deliberately in a desperate attempt to rid himself of the man on his trail.

He had failed. He had felt his pursuer's presence in that dry, canyon-cut land lying eternally patient under a baleful sun and had risked everything in a run through Apache country, gambling that a war party would cut off his pursuer. He did not know if he had been successful, and the thought prodded him into action.

He was almost home. The thought gave him a lift, and a thin smile crooked the alkali-raked corners of his mouth. He started across the shallow pool, but stopped as Felipe's gray, raising its head, whinnied after him.

The Kid studied the animal for a long moment; trailing after him, the animal could give him away. He slid his rifle out of the scabbard, levered a shell into place, raised the muzzle and fired quickly, wanting to get it over at once. The gray staggered and fell into the pool.

The Kid turned the piebald around and sent it jogging toward the distant, ragged hills.

An hour later the country began to rise. The spiky desert growth gave way to clumps of jack pine, swatches of hardy grass and granite outcroppings. Two hours later the piebald came to the edge of the Tenido Barrier, a volcanic fault that sheered off at the Kid's feet to drop two hundred feet straight down to the valley below. To the right and left of the Kid the Tenido Barrier ran for sixty-five miles, ending at the canyon of the Rio Grande at one end and fading into the Mescaleros at the other.

Below the Tenido Barrier lay Padre Valley.

The afternoon sun lay hot against his back as the Kid let his eyes take in the distant adobe blocks of the valley town of Avalon. It was an old town, older than Texas . . . older even than Mexico. It had been there, a cluster of Indian pueblos, when Cortez had come riding at the head of his mail-clad army across the Rio Grande.

The Kid could make out the gold cross atop the Mission of San Pablo, and his fancy brought to his ears the familiar tolling of the mission bell. His gaze moved on, following the windings of the Aztec Creek, glinting in the lowering sun. And though he could not see any of the buildings from where he sat, he knew that the big hacienda of Don Cambriano lay astride the upper Aztec. The Cambrianos, too, were older than Texas. . . .

The piebald stepped gingerly over the hard rimrock, leaving no discernible trace. But the Kid knew where he was going. Not more than two other men in Padre Valley knew the way into and out of the valley through the Tenido Barrier. And now one of them was dead.

The rift that appeared in the rimrock was a

crack that seemed to lead nowhere. But the Kid turned the piebald into the slit. The animal's shod hoofs slipped on the steep descent and the piebald sat on its haunches to keep from plunging over the edge. Below him the tops of cedars looked like wispy gray-green daubs on matchsticks.

The Kid jerked the piebald onto the narrow looping trail under the rock overhang that hid the trail from above, and the animal found the footing easier. This trail had been hewn out of the solid rock more than a hundred years before, by Indian laborers who had built the Mission. It was a trail for burros.

The sun beat him going down. The western rim of Padre Valley was in shadow when the Sonora Kid reached the bottom of the trail. With the coming of darkness the Kid felt a lift of his spirits. The pursuer he had spotted on his trail would be slowed down by the rimrock and the night.

He did not fool himself that his pursuer would not find the way down the Barrier. But the Sonora Kid wanted only enough time to get to Avalon.

He turned and ran his gaze up the dark and eternal bulk of the Barrier, and his smile had a thin-lipped insolence. "I don't know who you are," he whispered grimly. *"But this is my country. . . ."*

The piebald seemed to sense the end of the heart-breaking flight. He moved ahead in a fast jog, following a faint trail he and the rider knew instinctively. It was rough, sparsely-timbered land under the Barrier—land that sloped gently toward Aztec Creek and the old, old town of Avalon.

The Kid rode for more than an hour before he came to the tangled *bosque* rimming a feeder of Aztec Creek. Recent rains had run water through the small stream, and now the stars shone on the rocky bed, reflecting from shallow pools. The Kid started across, his eyes searching the far bank for old cattle paths through the brush.

The sudden warning snort from the shadows ahead raised the hackles on the Kid's neck. The piebald stopped abruptly, shivering, and the Kid's Colt slid into his hand. The shadows ahead of him moved, and a big steer walked into view. He was an immense brute with an enormous spread of horns. His tail was matted and his flanks were lean, his hips bony. Patches of his roan hide had rubbed off, giving him a mean and mangy look.

"*El Rojo*!" the Kid breathed. He fired the moment the outlaw steer came into sight, and he glimpsed a spurt of dust off the animal's hide, just behind the left ear. The Kid fired again, but the piebald was wheeling in fright as he pulled the trigger and he did not see the results of his second shot.

He gave the piebald its head, and the animal splashed across the shallow pools, hunched up the low bank where other cattle had beaten a path and pounded through the brush. The Kid buried his face in the piebald's coarse mane and let the animal run.

Ten minutes later the piebald had run itself out. He settled down to a leg-weary walk, and the Kid, looking back to the dark line of the *bosque*, muttered: "It was *El Rojo* himself!" He took a deep breath and crossed himself. There was a belief among the old people in Padre Valley that when a man was unfortunate enough to run across the big roan outlaw, the devil was not far behind!

Ahead of him the stage road from Saludad, on the Mexican side of the Rio Grande, swung in a wide loop that brought it to within a hundred yards of the *bosque*. The Kid had come that way before. He turned the piebald to the stretch of rocky ground between the edge of the brush and the stage road and dismounted.

The piebald was giving out. His head drooped and lather flanked his heaving sides.

"Just a few more miles," the Kid urged softly. "Then you'll get your rest."

With the blade of his hunting knife he pried off the worn shoes, placing them carefully in his saddle bags. This was his last trick. The grim nemesis on his trail knew the marks of those shoes by heart—would he distinguish the marks of the piebald's unshod hoofs from those of others in the dust of the stage road?

For good measure he used an old Apache trick. Roping a small bush, he pulled it up from its roots, and when he rode down off the rock outcropping onto the stage road, he dragged the bush over the piebald's tracks. He rode for about half a mile, mingling his tracks with the older ones on the road. Then he pulled in his rope, released the bush and tossed it aside. He rode on toward town. . . .

The moon cast a thin shadow as he rode into Avalon. The Kid wore his hat low over his eyes, and he rode slumped over his saddle horn. He came into Avalon along a narrow back street, past open doors that cast pale swatches of lamplight into the trampled, garbage-littered dust, past men lolling against dirty adobe walls, past wailing youngsters not ready for sleep. . . .

He crossed the main road, San Pablo Avenue, and midway into the next block he turned abruptly into an alley that led to the edge of town, and walked to a long adobe structure that served as both living quarters and barn and backed by a small pole corral.

The Kid dismounted, walked to the door at the end of the structure and pounded on it.

"Toreno!"

He waited impatiently, a dark, slim figure in the night. He heard movement behind the door; then it opened. A short, enormously fat Mexican in his late twenties filled the doorway. A smoky lamp cast its light against his back. His eyes widened as he saw the Kid.

The Kid shoved him back inside the dirty, garlic-smelling room before the fat man could open his mouth, and followed after him. "We must work fast, Toreno!" the Kid snapped. "There is someone following me—a lawman. He will come soon, maybe tonight. Tomorrow, most surely. You must get rid of my *caballo*!" He was starting to strip as he talked. "Saddle, bags, everything! Get rid of them!"

Toreno nodded. He started to turn, then looked back. "Felipe?" he began. "Where—?"

"Felipe is dead!" the Kid replied.

Toreno looked at him for a moment, troubled. Then he turned and dragged an iron-banded trunk from a small closet. "I kept them in here," he said to the Kid. He unlocked the trunk and took out a pair of green velveteen trousers, white-ruffled shirt, string tie, charro jacket, hand-tooled boots, pearl gray sombrero . . . the accounterments of a Spanish gentleman.

The Kid finished washing. "Your razor? It is sharp?"

"I was saving its edge for you," Toreno said. He watched the Kid shave and helped him get into the clothes he had laid out on his bunk. The difference they made was remarkable. The Sonora Kid was gone. In his place was a Spanish *caballero*. He seemed taller, assured. He belonged in Avalon.

The Kid fingered the small bullet cut under his left eye. Washing had loosened some of the scab, and it was oozing blood. He held a towel to it until it stopped bleeding. The cut wasn't serious, but it might call for some explaining.

Toreno held up the finishing touch to the Kid's transformation: a handsome leather cartridge belt, studded with silver; a fancy pearl-handled Colt in a tooled, embossed leather holster.

The Kid watched Toreno put his old belt and gun into the trunk, along with his old clothes, as he buckled on his new cartridge belt.

"Remember," he warned, "get rid of the piebald! And you have seen no stranger ride into town tonight! Eh, Toreno?"

The other grinned. His smile broadened as the Kid dropped a gold piece on his bunk. "But of course, *senor*—"

The flash of the Kid's eyes warned him.

Toreno nodded. "I have seen no stranger tonight. Of that I am certain!"

The Kid went outside, stopping by the spent piebald to retrieve the leather money bag. "The black mare? She is still in your stall?"

"*Si*!" Toreno stepped outside, hitching at his baggy pants. "She has grown fat since you've been away. I have not let her outside, as you said, except at night. Then I make her run around the corral."

"Saddle her!"

Ten minutes later the Kid rode out of the alley, mounted on a sleek black mare whose sires had been Barb and Arabian. He turned at the Avenue, and he did not ride far. Only as far as the big *plaza*, the square of San Pablo. He tied the black horse at the rack in front of the *El Toro Grande Cantina.* He did not go inside. He kept his eyes on the lighted window of the law office under the arcade across the square. He walked swiftly up the wide stone steps of the church, carrying his leather money bag.

The high-beamed interior was dark save for candles burning at the altar and one flickering quietly under the statue of the Virgin Mary.

Two old women, shrouded in black, knelt in the shadows of the middle pew, fingering their rosaries. They paid no attention to the Kid.

He walked to the altar rail, knelt and crossed himself. His silent prayer was a curious mixture of reverence and hate. In that moment hate was stronger than reverence . . . his hate extended, without qualification, to the entire state of Texas!

Rising, he went out by a small, vaulted side door. The moon was on the other side of the Mission, and he was in deep shadow. But the Kid didn't hesitate. He turned left, toward the small cemetery in the rear of the Church of San Pablo, and disappeared.

CHAPTER TWO

— The Bounty Hunter —

The sun was an hour high when Ben Craig came to the waterhole. He rode warily, a hard, dusty man with a grim face and quick-moving, alert eyes. All day yesterday he had seen signs of Apache war patrols. They were between him and the Sonora Kid, and he had half expected to find the Kid and his companion pincushioned by Apache arrows.

Instead he found Felipe sprawled facedown by the waterhole. A glance told him what had happened. Ben's gaze moved to the body of the gray horse lying half out of the water . . . then he picked up the Kid's trail, moving across the hard sandy soil toward the distant barrier, dark blue against the horizon.

The Tenido Barrier!

Ben had come that way before, but he knew of no way across the rock-bound fault at that point. But the Kid probably did, or he would not have come that way.

Ninety thousand dollars could keep a man living high for the rest of his life in Mexico. And the Kid had a good chance to get away with it. A Wells Fargo agent had authority that carried across state or territory lines, but he would get little cooperation across the Border.

Ben crossed back to his horse and started to mount. He hung there for a moment, his foot in stirrup, staring up at the southeastern sky where several buzzards were circling lazily. He waited, knowing what those ominous harbingers signified . . . something dead or dying below them!

Sam Jelco?

It was possible. The bounty hunter had been ahead of him all the way, closing in fast on the Kid. Then, last night, he had lost him.

Ben Craig eased up into his saddle; he sat still, caught between the impulse to ride on after the Kid or turn to the southeast. The devil with it! he thought, and started to ride away.

The rifle shots, sounding in the distance, held him again. They carried a note of desperate urgency across the barren desert. Someone was trapped out there; there was no doubt about it!

Ben swung his horse to the east, sliding his rifle across his saddle. . . .

Sam Jelco crouched in the rocks, using his teeth to knot the dirty handkerchief around the gash in the flesh of his right forearm. The grime and sweat of a long trail darkened his stubbled face; he stared, like a trapped and dangerous animal, over his arm to the hot, sandy clearing ahead.

It was not the sort of place he would have picked to end his thirty-eight years on earth.

Two Apaches lay sprawled, facedown, less than forty feet from him. He knew there were four others. But he couldn't see them. Somewhere in the jumble of rocks ahead he could make out their ponies, tied to a picket line. His own horse was dead somewhere behind him . . . he had managed to make it to this temporary shelter with only an arrow cut across his forearm.

Now he carefully weighed his last two rifle shells in the palm of his hand before sliding them into the magazine. His Colt was over by his horse, lost in his tumbling fall from the saddle. He had managed to hold onto his rifle . . . but he wished now that he had been able to keep his Colt.

He rocked forward as an Apache appeared less than a hundred yards in front of him. He fired instinctively and saw the bullet hit the brave. But the Apache came on, and he fired again, desperately. The warrior spun around and fell . . . and Sam looked down at his empty gun. He had time for one bleak moment of reflection; then the others came at him, gliding silently, closing in. . . .

He waited in the rocks, clutching the muzzle

of his rifle, ready to swing it as a club. He was a big man, solid muscles toughened by constant use. They'd have to come for him in there!

The shots from the ridge came fast, and the first two Apaches crumpled in their tracks. The other two, caught by surprise, headed for the rocks, not even trying to see who was firing. Only one Apache reached the sheltering boulders, and he was dying when he fell out of sight.

Sam faced the ridge, still grasping his rifle by the muzzle. It took a moment for him to realize what had happened . . . that his reprieve had come at the eleventh hour.

He waited, eyeing the man who showed up on the rocky slope above him, as Ben Craig came walking down, his rifle held across his waist, Sam reacted with narrowing gaze. He knew Ben Craig; they generally worked opposite ends of the law.

Sam leaned back against a rock, a thin smile on his lips. He had never known anything but trouble. . . . As a boy, orphaned early, he had been farmed out to relatives who were interested only in how much work they could get out of him. He had grown big and tough before he was fifteen. . . . He had joined the Army at sixteen, lying about his age, and after the Civil War he had joined Quantrill's Raiders, feeling he deserved more from his years with the Army than an honorable discharge. He had drifted naturally into the risky business of being a bounty hunter . . . the business of trapping the most dangerous game alive: Man.

He waited for Ben now, grateful, but only mildly so. . . . Had the shoe been on the other foot, he might have ridden on, for he knew Ben was after the Sonora Kid, too.

He reached into his vest pocket for the last of his Mexican cheroots and was lighting up as Ben arrived. He tossed his match aside and grinned. “What took you so long, Ben?”

Ben eyed him for a brief moment. The man’s gall was not unexpected. He shrugged and smiled faintly. “Got held up deciding.”

Sam frowned. “Deciding?”

Ben nodded. “Whether to pull you out of a hole or keep riding.”

Sam shook his head. “You had to come, Ben.” His grin widened. “Man with a conscience—”

“It can be strained!” Ben cut in. He picked up Sam’s hat, lying at his feet, and tossed it to him. “You after the Kid?”

Sam shrugged. “Aren’t you?”

Ben eyed him coldly. “It’s a Wells Fargo job, Sam. He’s got ninety thousand dollars . . . Wells Fargo money!”

Sam’s eyes widened; he blew out a breath of surprise. “That much, eh?”

“What are you after?” Ben asked.

Sam shrugged. "Bounty money . . . ten thousand dollars' worth." He eyed Ben for a moment. "Looks like we're after the same man, Ben. But I reckon I owe you something for this." He indicated the dead Apaches. "Let's make it a fair contest. If you get to the Kid first, I'll let him be."

"And if you get to him before me?" Ben asked coldly.

"He'll get a bullet between the eyes," Sam promised.

Ben stared at him for a brief moment; then he nodded. "Fair enough," he agreed coldly. He turned and started to walk away.

Sam took off after him. "Hey!" he protested. "Wait a minute!"

Ben turned to look at him.

"I'm out of shells," Sam said. "And I need a hoss—"

"There's five Apache ponies in the rocks," Ben cut in, pointing. "Might take you a little while to catch one, but—" he grinned—"you need the exercise, anyway. As for shells . . . ?" He shook his head. "Haven't any to spare. You'll just have to keep out of trouble until you reach town!"

"You agreed to a fair contest!" Sam howled.

"I didn't agree to outfit you," Ben answered. He smiled briefly. "See you in Avalon, Sam."

He turned and headed back up the ridge to

where he had left his horse. Sam stared after him, a belligerent scowl on his face. . . . Then he started walking slowly toward the rocks where the Apaches had left their horses.

It was past noon when Ben Craig arrived at the Tenido Barrier. Now his hard gaze picked up the far-off cluster of dwellings in the valley below; a neatly patterned community which seemed brushed by some painter's hand against the brown canvas of Padre Valley.

The sun was a burning ball in the brassy sky above him. Ben felt it against his back and ran his tongue over dry lips. He did not regret taking the time to help Sam Jelco; but it had given the Sonora Kid that much more of a start.

"The Kid's got a night jump on us," he muttered to his horse. "But I've got a hunch that town's where he was headed . . . not Mexico; not with those revolutionaries raising blazes along the Border right now. He's going to hole up in Avalon, at least until it's safe to cross over into Mexico."

The big animal under him moved restlessly. They had come a long way from Boxwood City, through mountains and desert, and it had fashioned a bond between them.

Thirsty now, the horse whickered his need.

Ben reached over to stroke his muzzle. "Ran out, feller. From now on in we ride dry." He lifted his glance to the valley below, his eyes narrowing.

Padre Valley. He had heard of the valley from hard-mouthed riders, but few seemed to know exactly where to place it. Somewhere beyond the Big Bend country, somewhere in that lost and lawless region of tumbled hills and lonely badlands, somewhere "*mas alla—*" on beyond.

Well, he had come upon it now. But the question was: How had the Kid gotten down the almost sheer drop?

Ben walked his horse slowly, following the tracks of the Kid's piebald. Those markings were burned in his head . . . he had been following them for almost seven hundred miles!

They led him to the crack in the Barrier, and he smiled at the still visible scars on the rock made by the piebald's sliding hoofs. He couldn't see much of a trail below him, but if the piebald had gone that way, his animal could follow.

Heading his horse into the break, Ben found the narrow burro trail under the overhang and followed it down the sheer face of the Tenido Barrier.

The sun was angling west when he hit the bottom of the trail. He picked up the Kid's tracks again and followed them to a small creek lying bright in the hot sun. He paused in the middle of the dry stream bed, studying the pattern of the piebald's markings. Something had stopped the Kid there, diverted his flight. The big Wells Fargo agent's eyes caught the gleam of a brass cartridge lying in the sand, and he bent sideways in the saddle and picked it up. A .45 shell. He put the cartridge casing in his pocket and rode over to the brush-choked bank where he spotted the sharp hoof marks of a steer. A big fellow, he thought—and it occurred to him that the Sonora Kid must be jumpy to spook and waste a shell on a stray steer.

He rode back and followed the piebald's trail through the tangled *bosque*, along an old steer path that cut like a tunnel through the spiky growth. He was just coming out of the brush when he heard a woman scream!

CHAPTER THREE

— Julia Cambriano —

The stage from Saludad made the trip to Avalon once a week. It was an old coach, for travel was not brisk between Padre Valley and Saludad, especially since Chico Montero and his band of ragged revolutionaries had made their headquarters in the hot hills just across the Rio Grande.

The driver, Jamato, was an old man. His companion on the seat was a squat, dumb-faced peon with three-quarters Yaqui blood in him. The man had paid his fare to Avalon, which was enough for Jamato, whose job was to handle the four-horse team and not ask questions. The breed rode up on the hot, dusty seat by preference, and this Jamato understood. The only other passengers were the *Senora* Julia Cambriano and her duenna, *Dona* Alcita. And peons did not ride in the company of such.

The coach rattled and bounced and squeaked, although Jamato drove at a sedate pace and endeavored to avoid all chuck-holes. Consequently, he was not so much surprised as irritated when he heard the cracking of wood and felt the coach suddenly sag behind him.

He hauled the team up short, wiped his sweaty brow and climbed down from his seat. It was fortunate, he thought, that this should happen a few miles short of his destination.

The coach door swung open and a girl stepped out. Her hat, a plumed velvet affair, was tilted over her face. One eye, black and alive with excitement, looked at Jamato, then turned to the rear of the coach. The wheel had folded inward, and the carriage rested on its weathered hub.

Jamato eyed the disaster with unhurried speculation. He heard a muttered exclamation from inside the coach, but he didn't bother to look around. *Dona* Alcita, clutching a rosary in one hand, emerged from the tilted carriage. She took a look at the wheel, and her sharp voice rose on the heated air, berating the driver, his obvious stupidity, and extending the accusation to include the criminally careless company which would employ such an old fool to drive such a dangerous piece of equipment.

Jamato took her beratement without comment. He had been married for forty years, and the words fell harmlessly on ears trained to disregard them. He walked to the wheel. The weakened spokes, he saw, had finally given way. He was glad it was the wheel, and not the axle, which had broken. For such an emergency he carried a spare wheel, fastened under the coach, and a stout length of seasoned oak to be used as a lever.

It was hot. The sun was always hot at that time of the year, he reflected. He turned and called to the dull-faced man on the seat. Jamato was glad the man was along. He looked strong as a bull and Jamato would have need of his strength.

Dona Alcita, having vented her irritation, ceased talking. She was a tall, stern-faced, pious woman whose sole duty was to accompany the daughter of Don Cambriano and see to it that she behaved in the approved fashion of a Spanish lady.

Julia Cambriano was a beautiful girl, and she had many admirers on both sides of the Border. It annoyed *Dona* Alcita that Julia seemed to prefer a certain gringo (*si*, *si*, that was the word for such!) on the Texas side of the Rio Grande.

Julia Cambriano was speaking to Jamato. "Will it take long?" she asked.

The old driver shrugged. "An hour, perhaps." He nodded toward the broad, squatty man climbing down from the seat. "If he is as strong as he looks, *senorita* . . . ?"

The girl looked around her. The road had made a wide loop, necessitated by a granite outcropping, and had brought it close to a stretch of *bosque* that hid the meanderings of a small creek. She frowned. Avalon, she knew, was only two hours away. But this road, coming from the south, was not heavily traveled—and her father's riders did not ordinarily come this far out of their way.

She resigned herself to waiting.

But Julia Cambriano was an active girl, slim and supple and full of good spirits. And although it was hot in the direct glare of the sun, and *Dona* Alcita bade Julia join her in the comparative coolness of the shade cast by the stage, she decided against it.

Reaching inside the tilted carriage, she fetched her white parasol, opened it and holding the long skirts of her traveling dress so she could walk more freely, turned to the *bosque.* The tangled matting of low trees and brush intrigued her. Old steer paths, like dim tunnels, wound through it—and its shade and quiet attracted her.

She had covered half the distance to the edge of the brush when a heavy snorting froze her. She clutched her parasol handle tightly, her eyes widening.

Directly ahead the immense horns and head of a big roan steer thrust into the sunlight, followed slowly by the ominous shoulders and matted flanks.

Julia screamed! Then she turned and ran, forgetting to hold up her long skirts. She covered fifteen feet before she tripped. Behind her

El Rojo, long tormented by the flies and gnats swarming about the bullet gash across his flank, saw the wildly waving parasol and charged!

Ben Craig took in the scene in one swift glance—the coach sagging in the middle of the road, the two men standing by the broken rear wheel, the Mexican woman coming around the back of the stage. . . .

His glance slid over this background scene and focused on the nearer, grimmer picture of a running girl holding a white parasol, who just then stumbled and fell. And between him and the girl was the big roan outlaw steer, needle-sharp horns held low as he charged!

There was no time for deliberation. The thought flashed through Ben's head that no .45 slug fired from that angle could hope to stop that enraged animal, and his palm fell away from the butt of his Colt even as his heels raked his horse's flanks.

His big stallion lunged ahead, sensing the urgent need for speed. A hundred yards separated the Wells Fargo agent from the girl—half of that between him and the outlaw steer.

The stallion caught up to *El Rojo* with less than twenty yards to spare. He ran alongside, like a trained rodeo bronco ready to drop his rider in a bulldogging contest. And the Wells Fargo man did just that.

He dropped alongside the roan steer, his hands closing on the wide spread of horn. The girl was scrambling to her feet, directly in their path. He slammed with all his strength in a violent, twisting hug that almost broke the big steer's neck. *El Rojo* stumbled; one horn hooked into the dirt, and the momentum of his charge slammed his nose into the ground. His hindquarters, twisting inward, flipped up. He landed on his back with a jarring thud.

Ben whirled away, the sleeve of his right hand slit to the elbow, blood oozing from a shallow gouge along his muscular forearm. His horse was five feet away. Ben stepped quickly into the saddle and whirled the big stallion.

Julia Cambriano was still on her hands and knees, a most undignified position for a girl of her breeding, when Ben leaned out of his saddle. His right arm encircled her waist. She felt herself plucked off the hot ground almost effortlessly and brought across the stallion's saddle just as the big roan steer, shaking his head, scrambled to his feet.

Ben wheeled the stallion. Most of the fight had been knocked out of *El Rojo*. Ben drew his Colt. His first bullet, intentionally aimed, kicked up a spurt of dust under the outlaw steer's nose—the second nicked its left ear.

Snorting heavily, *El Rojo* wheeled and sought the sanctuary of the dark *bosque*.

Ben watched him go. He was thinking that this roan outlaw must have been the animal that had spooked the Kid and received a bullet across its flank the night before.

He turned his attention to the girl in the curve of his arm. She lay against his chest, her eyes closed, and he wondered if she had fainted. He could feel the steady beat of her heart, and the faint odor of a light perfume brought back a memory of another girl and another time.

She stirred then, and he asked gently: "Are you hurt?"

She shook her head. "Only my pride," she answered. She turned her face to him, and he saw she was young and pretty. Shock had drained some of the blood from her cheeks, but he saw that she had recovered quickly. Lights were already dancing in her dark eyes, and a small smile started to play around her full-lipped mouth.

She turned and looked down to where her parasol lay, and Ben rode to it, dismounted and retrieved it for her. She held it over her head, color back in her cheeks. "Thank you, *senor*," she said gratefully. "My duenna will give me a devil of a scolding. But I will return to the coach, at least, in the manner she thinks befits the daughter of Don Cambriano."

Ben mounted behind her. The tiny parasol

cast a spot of shade over both of them as he turned his stallion to the stage. A grin touched Ben's lips at the picture he presented.

Julia Cambriano was right about the scolding. *Dona* Alcita started her tongue lashing before Ben eased Julia down by the coach. The shock of what might have happened to her charge had completely unnerved the old duenna, and she took out her hysteria on the girl.

Julia ignored the outburst, understanding the reason for it. She turned and looked up at Ben, seeing a tall man with a stubble of reddish brown beard roughening a strong face. He was a man who had come a long way, who had slept little—yet he gave the impression of tireless energy. Julia Cambriano was young, yet she had a mature woman's intuition. And in that quick appraisal, she sensed a loneliness and a purpose in this rider that tantalized her.

"It was *El Rojo*, that outlaw steer," she explained. "He is a legend in Padre Valley." Her eyes darkened. "But why he should have tried to attack me—"

"He had a bullet slash across his ribs, and the flies must have been driving him crazy," Ben said evenly. "So he lay in wait in the brush, nursing his hate, and when you walked up he was ready to take that hate out on you."

The girl shuddered. Then: "Still, I am glad you did not kill him, *senor*—"

"Ben Craig, Miss," the Wells Fargo man supplied. His smile was noncommittal. "From points north—and heading south."

Behind the girl *Dona* Alcita said something in fluent Spanish. Ben grinned. "Reckon your duenna doesn't approve of me, Miss Cambriano."

The girl smiled. "She approves of no one who cannot trace his ancestry back to Spain; least of all a tall gringo stranger."

"And you?"

Julia shrugged. "My family, the Cambrianos, trace their lineage back to Castile. But I was born in Texas, as was my brother Carlos. I am a Texan, *senor.* And though I have many friends across the Rio Grande, I feel equally at home in Austin."

Ben nodded, his eyes appreciative. "You would be at home in any society," he said bluntly. Then, lifting his gaze to the two scowling men by the broken wheel, he said: "If I can be of help—?"

The girl turned to Jamato. She repeated Ben's offer in Spanish, but the old man shook his head. Watching, Ben sensed the hostility of both of the men.

Julia turned back to him. "I wish to thank you, *Senor* Craig. And though my duenna, *Dona* Alcita may not give you that impression, I do not hold my life lightly."

The Wells Fargo man smiled. "The pleasure

of helping you was all mine, *senorita*." He touched his hat brim politely. "*Adios*."

Julia watched him turn and ride up the road; then she faced the older woman, her face stern. "It was rude of you, *Dona* Alcita!" she censured her. "After all, he did save my life!"

The older woman's mouth tightened harshly. "He is a gringo!" she said unrelentingly. "One by one they come to take over this land that has been stained with our blood, this country we wrested from the ignorant savages. We were here first, Julia—"

"Sh!" the girl silenced her. "You have listened to my brother Carlos too long. This is not Mexico. This is Texas, and we, too, now are Texans. We would be happier to accept that, *Dona* Alcita. Already there is too much trouble because some of us will not remember that."

The older woman turned away from the girl, her eyes following the big rider fading on the hot road to Avalon.

She was remembering the way he had handled the big roan steer, and the words of the prophecy came into her thoughts and she shivered. "He is tall and has green eyes," she muttered, clutching her rosary, "and he rides with a big gun on his thigh."

In the hot sunlight she crossed herself quickly, the beads clicking softly in the stillness.

CHAPTER FOUR

— Soothsayer of Death —

Ben Craig came to Avalon at the tail end of the siesta hour. He had lost the Kid's trail back at the point where he had left the Saludad stage, and though he made several excursions on both sides of the road, he did not cut the piebald's sign again.

Nor had he expected to. Behind this tall Wells Fargo agent were years spent following signs and he had immediately noticed the rake-like furrows in the road that started at the point where a stretch of rocky ledge intersected it. Ben Craig's lips had crinkled. The Sonora Kid was using Apache tricks to cover his trail.

He followed the brush marks until they ended abruptly. Then Ben got down and studied the prints in the road. Among the dozen older ones three caught his attention; three which he guessed had been made during the night or early morning.

One was that of a small burro, which he dismissed. The other two he studied carefully.

One set of hoofprints indicated a shod horse. But the markings were not those of the piebald he had tracked for seven hundred miles. The other was the set of an unshod horse.

This left him two possibilities to consider. One: the Kid had carried a set of shoes in his saddle bag for just such an emergency and had cold-ironed them in place of the piebald's worn plates. Or: the Kid had ripped off the old shoes and ridden into town on a shoeless animal.

Ben decided to follow the shoeless cayuse. He followed the tracks until they parted from the others on the edge of town and came up a back street, across San Pablo Avenue, and down the alley to the adobe structure on the outskirts of Avalon.

A fat, sloppy Mexican was dozing in the shade of a tall pecan by the corral. A huge anthill sombrero was tilted over the man's face, its brim resting on the bulge of his large stomach. He didn't awaken as Ben rode up, but one hand rose slowly and slapped ineffectually at a half-dozen green bottle flies which buzzed around his ear.

Ben rested his forearms on his saddle horn and surveyed the scene. The dispirited horses crowded the corral bars behind the sleeping man. Both werc dun-colored animals seeking relief from the sun in the scant shade that fell on their side of the corral.

After a long moment of silence Ben

dismounted. He walked to the open door facing him at the end of the long adobe building and looked inside. An old shotgun hung on pegs over an untidy bunk. Ben's nose crinkled at the powerful odor of fried chile and garlic. The small room was obviously inhabited by the fat man resting under the pecan.

The Wells Fargo agent walked back, stood over the dozing stable keeper, then changed his mind. He walked to the corral, climbed over the bars, and made his way across the manure-littered ground to the partially opened barn door which made up one section of the enclosure.

The barn was sectioned off into six stalls and a space for storing hay and feed. Two of the stalls were occupied, one by a raw-boned gray stud with a mean look in its eyes; the other by a small, barrel-bellied brown mare.

He could see, without looking any closer, that there was no place left where a piebald horse could be hidden.

Ben turned back. He was halfway across the enclosure when his attention was caught by a small cold forge and anvil in the shade of the pecan inside the corral. Anvil, forge and a small wooden water trough were set against the building wall where the pole fence made a corner.

He turned for a closer look. But a soft ingratiating voice stopped him. The voice said:

"*Perdone*, *amigo*. You are looking for a fresh *caballo*, *si*?"

Ben swung around. The fat Mexican was on his feet, standing against the corral bars. He was smiling with obsequious friendliness. But the muzzle of the ancient shotgun had a cold and almost brutal directness.

A faint surprise, tinged with respect, flickered through the Wells Fargo man. He had not heard the fat man at all; yet the man had gone inside his room and returned before Ben had come out of the barn!

Craig walked back to the corral, passing a foot from the shotgun muzzle. "You greet all your customers this way?" he queried evenly.

Toreno shrugged. "A precaution, *senor.* One never knows. . . ." He lifted his huge shoulders, but he did not withdraw the gun muzzle.

Ben nodded. "You were asleep. I did not wish to disturb a man so happily engaged." He grinned.

Toreno's eyes crinkled. "I am most assuredly awake now, *senor*," he pointed out. "Is there somethin' I can do for you?"

Ben put his hands on the bars and climbed over, ignoring the shotgun. Toreno took a step backward. "*Si*, *senor*?" His tone was insolently respectful.

"I am looking for a horse," Ben said bluntly, "a big piebald stallion. I think he was ridden in here by a man who had taken off his shoes—a man who rode into town sometime during the night."

Toreno frowned. "Such an animal, *senor*, I have not seen. Nor any stranger. But—" his eyes brightened with quick avarice— "if you wish, I have two nice *caballos* inside the barn which I will be most happy to trade for your—" he turned, eyeing Ben's big stallion with unconcealed admiration—"for your worn-out mount, *senor*."

Ben's lips tightened coldly. He reached inside his pocket and brought out a twenty-dollar gold piece which he slowly and carefully balanced on the muzzle of the shotgun. "I will add five more of these for news of that piebald, and the man who rode him."

The fat Mexican studied the gold coin with grave deliberateness. "*Senor*," he said finally, "I would gladly lie for five more of such as this." His heavy shoulders lifted again. "But I am afraid you would be most unhappy, no?"

Ben shrugged. "One of us would be very unhappy," he admitted evenly. He stepped past the man and climbed into his saddle. He was sure of one thing. The piebald had been ridden there, which meant that the Sonora Kid was still in town; also that the Kid had friends in Avalon—a possibility he had given little thought to until that moment.

He glanced back as he rode through the alley. The fat Mexican was still standing with the gold coin balanced on the barrel of his shotgun.

Ben Craig turned his buckskin east on San Pablo Avenue and followed the wide cobbled thoroughfare to the big *plaza* surrounded on three sides by old, three-storied adobe buildings. The outside walls of these structures extended over the sidewalks, supported by fan-shaped pillars of whitewashed masonry. Under these archways vendors had set up shop.

Facing Ben, in the center of the hot plaza, a stone statue of Cortez, mounted on a rearing stallion, endured the sun with stolid indifference. Pigeons roosted on the old *Conquistadore's* sword arm. The inscription in the base of the statue read: "*Por Dios y Espana*—for God and Spain."

Beyond the statue, large against the hot sky, was the mission of San Pablo. Broad stone steps led up to massive double doors of solid oak planking, held in place by huge bronze hinges. The doors of San Pablo were never closed, the dimly lighted interior offering its sanctuary and its peace to all who wished to partake of them.

The Wells Fargo agent rode to within a dozen paces of the statue, letting his glance linger on a group of men watching a lithe, bright-skirted girl dancing barefooted to the beat of a tambourine and guitar. She was not more than fifteen—yet her figure was well developed and her eyes, meeting his, were bold and inviting.

Ben eased forward over his saddle horn. He had a three days' growth of beard and he did not look prepossessing. And the gun on his hip, in a thonged-down black leather holster, spoke a plain warning.

The music faded away and the girl paused while a small boy in ragged pants passed a straw hat around the small group of men. A few dropped coins into it. He came shuffling up to Ben, his brown face cracking with a hesitant smile. Ben tossed a half-dollar into the hat, and the boy bowed, turned and scampered quickly back to the girl, holding the silver coin between his fingers for her to see.

Ben's gaze moved past the girl, rested on the man standing against one of the arcade pillars. In the marketplace setting the man stood out sharply, like a fifth ace in a deck of cards. He was a blond man, bareheaded, in his mid-twenties; a powerfully built man, thick-shouldered and bull-necked. He stood watching the dancer, a brown paper *cigarillo*, unlighted, dangling from his lips.

He wore one gun, a Remington .44, Ben noticed. The muzzle was jammed into his waistband above his right hip. But the butt was tilted for a left-hand draw.

The blond man's eyes met Ben's, then drifted off. He didn't move, nor did he light the cigaret in his mouth. He was there—waiting!

Behind Ben a thin, cracked voice wheedled, "Your fortune, *senor*? Let me tell you what your palm reveals. . . ."

He turned and looked down on an old, bent woman who had come to stand by his stirrup. The lines in her brown face were caused by the erosion of time—she could have been eighty. But time had not yet dulled the shiny black eyes that met his. A thin, fragile hand reached up to grasp Ben's.

"One peso, *senor.* That is little enough to pay for having one's future traced out for one, no?"

Ben Craig shrugged. He let the old woman take his hand. He felt her fingers move like dry reeds across his palm. Her voice singsonged softly in the plaza heat.

"The heart line—it is broken too soon, *senor.* You are a lonely man . . . but it is your destiny. . . ."

Ben listened with but half an ear, seeing the blond man stir now, his yellow eyes coming to rest on him again. The man's gaze was narrowing.

The fortuneteller's voice sank lower in its

mumble. ". . . the life line, ah, this is a long one, *senor.* But there's a line that crosses it here, one that threatens. . . ." Her fingers pressed against his palm, and Ben felt the hard coolness of a foreign object. The woman's mumble did not change, but her words came swiftly now. "Don't look, *senor.* Keno's watching. The man you want will be in the walled garden, behind the *Corrida de Toros* cantina. Show this to the one-eyed man behind the bar tonight, and he will let you inside. At ten tonight. . . ."

The blond man dropped his cigaret and spat out bits of tobacco.

Ben kept his eyes on him. His hand closed over the metal object the old woman had pressed into his palm. Without looking at it he dropped it into his coat pocket.

The soothsayer droned: "A peso, *senor.* . . ."

Ben dropped a coin into her outstretched hand, and she backed away, bowing and mumbling: "*Gracias*, *senor—muchas gracias*."

The blond man was coming through the group watching the dancer, shouldering them aside with confident rudeness. He came out into the full beat of the sun, and his eyes, slitting against the intense heat, took on the yellow glare of a big cat's.

He drifted to a halt beside Ben's right stirrup, a young and powerful man confident in his ability to handle himself.

"Nice hoss," he began. "Own it?"

They were all the same, Ben reflected bleakly. They were fast, and they had killed their man—and now they walked around with a chip on their shoulder. He looked down into the blond man's eyes, his own veiled and distant.

"From hocks to ears," he murmured.

The gunman's grin had the cruel laziness of a cat playing with a mouse. "Name's Kane," he said. "Jesse Kane."

He said the name as though it should mean something to Ben, as though he were sure it would mean something to anyone coming into Padre Valley.

Ben's voice was dry. "It's your name," he conceded.

Kane's yellow eyes flared. "Reckon it is, stranger—laid plain on the table." The smile had gone from his face. He ran his gaze over Ben, sliding over the plain warning of the thonged-down Peacemaker.

"A big man on a buckskin horse," he sneered. "We've been waitin' for you, Rick, for three days!"

Ben frowned, not understanding this. "Glad I was expected," he answered coldly.

Kane reached up to take the buckskin's bridle. "Fancy-lookin' cayuse for a two-bit gun runner," he said nastily. "I'm puttin' in my claim for him right now."

Ben's voice was soft, yet as deadly as steel sliding through oiled leather, cutting through the man's words. "Take your hands off him, Kane!"

The blond man's hard face lifted to Ben. "You make me, Rick!" he challenged harshly. He yanked on the buckskin's bit reins and at the same time jerked his left hand to the Remington pistol stuck in his waistband.

It was a fast draw. He got the Remington free just as Ben's booted toe collided with his jaw. Kane's head snapped back and his hands came up in a reflex, balancing motion. His Remington went off, blasting skyward, just as Ben's second kick sent the gun spinning from his hand.

The first kick would have dropped a lesser man. Kane braced himself on widespread feet, shook his bullet head, and his eyes cleared just as Ben slid out of the saddle. He balled his fists and lunged at the tall Wells Fargo agent, his lips drawing back in an animal snarl.

His eyes were clear, but not clear enough to see the iron fist that rammed into his mouth, breaking off two uppers and loosening three more. He faltered, reaching out with clawed fingers for the man in front of him. The bells of San Pablo seemed to be ringing in his ears. Then all at once the bells stopped and a great darkness descended over Jesse Kane.

He only vaguely felt himself falling. He landed on the small of his back, and though his eyes remained partially open, he didn't see a thing. . . .

CHAPTER FIVE

— The Man from Harvard —

A cynical voice from the direction of the arcade behind Ben said: "I told Jesse he would run into that sort of thing some day."

Ben turned, his back against the buckskin's flank, his eyes narrowing against the glare of the sun.

A tall man, as tall as Ben, stepped out of the arcade shadows fifty feet away. He had a long grave face and sober gray eyes. But he could not have been much older than Kane. He was of a wiry strength, and the way he held his Colt told the Wells Fargo man that he had spent a lot of time with it. And, if the badge on the tall man's clean white shirt meant anything, it also told Ben he was entitled to use the gun.

Ben waited quietly while the tall lawman, looking cool and unruffled in a black string tie, clean gray Stetson and neatly pressed gray pants tucked into shiny half-boots, walked over to him.

Waiting, Ben tried to puzzle the thing out. He had been expected, Kane said. That was strange, for the only man who knew he was coming, other than Sam Jelco who was behind him, was the Sonora Kid. Neither Kane nor this lawman tallied with the meager description he had of the Kid.

Ben Craig eyed the gun in the lawman's hand. "Someone made a mistake," he said evenly. "I just arrived in town."

"Isn't that true of all of us?" the other murmured. His voice was soft and pleasant; he spoke like an educated man not too far removed from books and lecture halls.

"I'm Archibald Rankin," he said. "Harvard—class of '71." There was no smile in his eyes. "My friends call me Arch. You can call me sheriff."

Ben frowned. "I'll call you when I need you," he said bluntly. He started to turn, ignoring the gun in the man's hand, when a shot blasted sharply across the heat of the plaza!

A rosary of dried chile, hanging from the arcade wall nearby, shook violently as the bullet tore through it.

Ben whirled. Ten feet away Jesse Kane was staring at his bloodied hand, his Remington at his feet.

Ben's gaze shifted quickly from the gunman to the lithe young Mexican moving slowly toward them from a cantina on the west side of the plaza. Huge block letters were painted in black over the cantina archway: CORRIDA DE TOROS.

The Mexican joined Ben and the sheriff in front of the statue of Cortez, a slender handsome Mexican, holding a gun with smoke coming from its muzzle. There was a two-inch scab under his left eye.

"Ordinarily, *senor*," he began pleasantly, "I do not intrude into quarrels among—shall we say?—gringos. But a shot in the back is hardly—" He glanced at Sheriff Rankin, his white teeth showing in a quick smile— "hardly sporting. Is that not so, Sheriff?"

Rankin's tone held a strange bitterness. "I didn't know you were back in Padre Valley, Carlos."

The Mexican shrugged. "I got tired of books and stuffy professors, Sheriff. There is much excitement in the land, too much for one to listen to ancient history."

Ben stood between the two men, a frown on his face. Kane started to pick up his gun, and the Wells Fargo agent shifted, his right hand dropping to his Colt butt in a naked warning.

The sheriff's voice rang out sharply. "Kane—leave it lay! Get the Doc to examine your hand; then meet me in the office!"

Ben's voice was bleak. "A real watchdog, Sheriff. You always sick him on strangers coming into Avalon?"

"Only when they come into town bringing trouble," the sheriff said coldly. His gaze moved to the young Mexican. "You return at a bad time, Carlos."

Ben extended his hand to the man. "You came back at a good time for me, just now," he said gratefully.

Carlos gripped the Wells Fargo agent's hand. "*Senor*— any man who is no friend of the sheriff's is a friend of mine."

Ben's grin turned crooked. "Thanks," he said dryly.

Carlos gestured across the square to a clean-limbed black mare nosing the cantina rail. "I was about to ride home—to my father's hacienda further up the valley. It would please me and my father to have you as our guest."

Ben hesitated. He had come seven hundred miles to get the Sonora Kid; not to be a guest at someone's hacienda, however pleasant the stay might be.

Sheriff Rankin's bitter voice said: "You show strange taste in picking your friends, Carlos!"

Carlos laughed. "Not as strange as the deputies you hire, Sheriff." He turned to Ben, sheathing his gun in a fancy, stitched-leather holster. "Come, *senor.* It is hot in the plaza—"

Behind them wheels rattled on the ancient cobblestones as the stage from Saludad came into the square. The old coach came to a stop in front of the small stage office. The driver climbed down from his seat and opened the door for the two women passengers.

Carlos' voice rang with sharp surprise. "*Senor* —wait! It is my sister, Julia!"

The two women paused in front of the office while the driver, followed by the powerful Yaqui breed, disappeared inside. Carlos' hailing voice turned them to the plaza.

Julia waved her hand and started toward them. *Dona* Alcita hesitated, then followed.

"Carlos!" the girl greeted him. "When did you get back? Did you get my letter?"

He shook his head. "No letter. I returned last night—rode all the way." He frowned. "And you? What brought you to Saludad?"

"I was hoping to meet you," she replied. Her troubled eyes moved to Ben Craig, and surprise made a faint quirk in her face.

Carlos said: "I am losing my manners, Julia. This is *Senor*—" He paused, shaking his head ruefully.

"Ben Craig," the Wells Fargo man supplied quietly.

Julia smiled. "I have met the *Senor* Craig, Carlos." Her eyes darkened as they moved to Sheriff Rankin, who was turning away. "Arch, aren't you glad to see me?"

"Always," the tall lawman said gallantly. "But I reserve my right to object to the company your brother keeps."

Julia bit her lips. She stared after Rankin, a hurt expression in her eyes. Carlos took her arm. "Come, Sis," he said roughly. "I've invited Ben to stay with us. Father will be glad to have him."

Julia turned to Ben, a flush spreading across her face. "I'm afraid Sheriff Rankin is letting his troubles make him forget him manners, Ben."

"Don't apologize for him, Sis!" Carlos cut in angrily. The young Cambriano didn't like the sheriff and he showed it; and he could be dangerous to anyone he didn't like, Ben thought.

"I've found most sheriffs have a right to be suspicious," he said, trying to ameliorate the situation. "Perhaps Mr. Rankin has more than his share of troubles here—"

The girl flashed him a grateful look, but Carlos cut in sarcastically: "Mr. Rankin has a great talent for avoiding trouble, Ben. But come; let us forget the *Senor* Rankin. I'll make arrangements for a carriage. I'm sure Julia won't mind entertaining you until my return. You are our guest, you know."

Julia was frowning as her brother walked off, his stride arrogant and quick. Ben said: "It's pleasanter in the shade. Shall we?"

They walked to the protection of the awninged walk in front of the stage office. The squat Yaqui who had been a passenger with the girl and her duenna was standing in the doorway, picking his teeth with a broom straw. His black eyes surveyed the women, then shifted to the tall Wells Fargo agent. He met Ben's glance without expression, nor did he look away until he had completed his bold appraisal. Then he picked up his goatskin bag and started to walk toward the *Corrida de Toros*.

Julia said: "You have business in Padre Valley, *Senor* Craig?"

"You might call it that," Ben answered. His hesitation was brief. "I'm looking for a man known as the Sonora Kid."

"The Sonora Kid?" Julia's brows knitted. "I've never heard of anyone by that name here. And I know almost everyone in the valley, all except—" She made a small gesture across the square, and Ben, turning, saw two riders coming down the big thoroughfare that led to the Plaza de Cortez.

They were hard men, whose guns shouted a cold warning from holsters thonged low on their thighs. They turned to a tierack in front of a dirty yellow building whose sign Ben could read from where he stood:

THE MAVERICK'S HANGOUT

Julia's voice was bitter. "There is the trouble of Padre Valley, Ben; also my father's troubles.

A man who calls himself Cal Stetson owns the place. He fancies himself a gentleman—"

Carlos appeared out of a side street, driving a carriage with a fringed canvas canopy protecting the seat from the beat of the hot sun. His black trotted alongside.

"If this man you call the Sonora Kid is a newcomer to the valley," the girl went on hurriedly, "it is quite possible you will find him among the men who frequent that place." She gave him a quick, searching look. "Is he a friend of yours?"

"Hardly." Ben's voice was dry. "But I am anxious to meet up with the man—"

"Who?" Carlos' voice was bright, almost gay, as he hauled the matched bays in close to the walk. "Whom would you like to meet, Ben?"

"Someone called the Sonora Kid," Ben answered levelly.

Carlos' brow puckered in thought. "I have been away at school these past years," he said. "It may be someone who has come to Padre Valley in that time. I do not know such a man, Ben." His teeth showed white against his brown face. "But then, Ben, many strangers have come to Padre Valley since I first went away to school . . ." His voice faded on a flat note as he glanced toward The Maverick's Hangout. Then he shrugged and swung down from the carriage.

"Julia, you can drive," he suggested quickly. "I'd like to ride alongside *Senor* Craig."

He helped his sister up into the seat while Ben gave *Dona* Alcita a hand. Carlos glanced admiringly at Ben's buckskin. "You wouldn't think of a horse trade, would you?"

Ben shook his head.

He swung up into the saddle, and as he wheeled his big stallion he saw Rankin standing in the shadow of the arcade across the plaza. Ben frowned. He had come into Padre Valley on the trail of the Senora Kid—and ninety thousand dollars of Wells Fargo money. Now he found himself getting involved in something he had not reckoned with. And behind him was Sam Jelco, a man with a quick gun and a one-track mind, to add to his troubles.

Still, Ben thought, if he expected to get a line on the Kid before Sam, he'd have to find out what the trouble here was about. For the Wells Fargo man was beginning to have a strong hunch that the Sonora Kid had not come into Padre Valley on a whim. The Kid had a reason. And Ben suspected that the Kid's motives were tied up with happenings in Padre Valley . . . the trouble that seemed to weigh so heavily on the educated shoulders of Arch Rankin.

CHAPTER SIX

— The Second Man —

Sam Jelco came to Avalon at sundown—a big rough-bearded man riding an Indian pony on which he had put his saddle, stripped from his dead horse. It had taken him an hour to catch up with one of the Apache ponies, another to find the way down the Barrier. But like Ben he tracked like an Apache. He had followed the piebald's tracks and Ben's, noting where Ben had bulldogged the steer. He had reconstructed fairly accurately what had happened . . . and he had not been entirely fooled by the Sonora Kid's ruse in trying to cover his tracks.

He was several hours behind Ben, and this did not sit well with him. The Sonora Kid was his quarry; he did not like sharing him with any man.

Ten thousand dollars was a lot of bounty money. But Sam Jelco was shooting for higher stakes: for ninety thousand dollars and a fast run across the Border. . . .

So impatience rode him with a naked rowel as he pulled up at the alley down which Ben had ridden earlier. The shadows were deep in the plaza's southwest side, and he did not notice

Rankin as the sheriff stepped out of his office and paused to look in his direction. He was intent on one thing . . . to get a lead on what Ben had found out concerning the piebald.

He turned up the alley, coming quickly to Toreno's adobe dwelling and his small corral and barn. He sat for a moment in the saddle, his gaze taking quick inventory. The two horses in the corral didn't interest him, but the barn did. Like Ben, he wanted a look inside.

He dismounted, tied his cayuse to the corral bars and started to climb over the fence. Toreno's soft, lazy voice stopped him.

"You wish to buy a horse, *senor*?"

He remained facing the barn across the corral, his back to Toreno. Sam had spent too many years tracking men not to recognize the danger in Toreno's voice . . . the lazy softness did not fool him.

Still not turning, he said: "I'm broke, fella. But I'll consider a trade."

Toreno came up behind him, standing close. His shotgun was held idly, its muzzle pointing at Sam's back. It gave him a sense of security and made him careless.

"You ride a poor animal, *senor*. I'm afraid I have nothing I would trade—"

He hardly saw Sam turn. Coming up close, he had little freedom of movement. Before he could thumb back the shotgun hammer, Sam's hand had batted the muzzle aside. He didn't see the muzzle of Sam's Colt as it jammed violently into his stomach, a few inches above his belt buckle.

Toreno gasped, bent over, and his nerveless hands dropped the shotgun. He staggered forward, clutched at the corral bars for support and clung there, fighting to get his breath back.

Sam picked up the shotgun and tossed it into the corral. Then he sheathed his Colt and faced Toreno. He waited until Toreno's breath came back; then:

"I'm figgerin' on a trade, Fat Boy. My pony for the worn-out piebald you got in that barn!"

Toreno straightened slowly, a sharp gleam in his eyes. He shook his head, his voice laboring. "A brown mare . . . inside. But no piebald . . ."

Sam slipped his Colt free again, thumbed back the hammer. He pointed the muzzle at Toreno's middle. "I tracked a piebald here, mister. Now if he ain't in that barn, *where is he?*"

Toreno eyed Sam's gun muzzle with bitter resignation. "Somewhere you have made a mistake, *senor.* I have seen no *caballo* such as you describe. It is what I have told the other stranger—"

"Ben was here?"

Toreno shrugged. "He did not speak his name. But, like you, he was askin' about a piebald horse." Toreno shook his head. "I have seen no such animal, *senor*!"

"You're a liar!" Sam said coldly.

Toreno stiffened. "*Senor—*"

"The name's Sam Jelco!" Sam snapped. "An' I don't give a hang about the piebald hoss. He's yores, if you have him." He eyed Toreno, measuring his greed against a possible friendship with the Kid. "It's the piebald's rider I'm after . . . an outlaw named the Sonora Kid."

Toreno's gaze dropped to Sam's gun; he grimaced uncomfortably. "You are a lawman, *Senor* Jelco?"

Sam laughed humorlessly. "Somethin' like that," he said. "A lawman minus a badge, and without a lawman's scruples—"

"Bounty hunter?" Rankin's voice was cold, stabbing out of the alley darkness behind Sam.

Sam started to turn, but remembered the gun in his hand and how the action might be misconstrued. The man in the alley had all the advantage. So he took a breath, slowly slid his Colt back into its holster, then made his turn, his manner unhurried, obviously peaceful.

He saw Rankin step slowly out of the shadows and come toward him. His glance picked up the badge on Rankin's coat, dropped quickly to the gun on Rankin's hip, then rested on Rankin's face. He was glad he had not turned on first impulse, with a gun in his hand.

Rankin stopped a few paces away, his glance

raking Toreno with little pleasure, locking on Sam.

"Bounty hunter?" he repeated.

Sam nodded slowly, his lips quirking. "Not an illegal profession, Sheriff. Or is there a law against them in Padre Valley?"

"No law," Rankin said coldly, "for or against your kind." His glance slid to Toreno, who had assumed the pose of a mistreated peon, suffering silently. He kept his glance on Toreno, but his question was to Sam. "Whom are you looking for here?"

Sam scowled. "Whom?" Then: "Oh, you mean who."

Rankin smiled coldly. "Yeah, who?"

"The Sonora Kid," Sam growled. He eyed Rankin closely, expecting some reaction. Getting none, he added: "Held up a train way north of here . . . got away with a saddlebag full of money."

Rankin frowned. "What are you after—the money or the bounty?"

Sam smiled thinly. "Now you know better than that, Sheriff."

"I know better," Rankin said pointedly. "But do you?"

Sam tightened slightly at the lawman's tone; then he shrugged. "All I'm after is the Kid," he said harshly. "The money he stole belongs to Wells Fargo."

Rankin looked at Toreno. "Do you know this Sonora Kid?"

Toreno shook his head violently, glad of an opportunity to speak. He spoke English quite well, but he preferred to lapse into the Spanish of the peons when addressed by Rankin. His denial was profusely sprinkled with complaints of mistreatment by Sam.

Sam caught enough to know what was going on. "He's a three-hundred-pound liar!" Sam said flatly. "That piebald was ridden up this alley by the Sonora Kid last night—"

Rankin cut him off. The sheriff had a more disturbing problem facing him than some outlaw the bounty hunter was after. "Maybe," he said to Sam. "But he could have cut across to the lot behind The Maverick's Hangout."

Sam looked hard at him. "The what?"

"Saloon run by a man called Cal Stetson. If your man's on the run from the law up north, you might find him in there. You might even find," he added humorlessly, "two or three others worth your time."

Sam's voice was level. "I work at one job at a time, Sheriff." He turned to Toreno. "I'll pay two hundred dollars, American gold eagles, for a line on the Kid."

Toreno shrugged. "Even if you had the money, *senor*, I could not tell you."

Sam's mouth tightened; he turned back to

Rankin. "All right, Sheriff. I'll take a look at The Maverick's Hangout." He sneered openly at Toreno. "I figgered the Kid was on the run for Mexico. But if he's got your kind of friends here, then he's still in Avalon. And if he is, Fat Boy, I'll get him!"

He turned away, untied his pony, mounted and rode down the alley without looking back.

Toreno plucked a large coarse handkerchief from his pocket and wiped his brow. "A bad one, that one," he said to Rankin. "I am grateful to you, Sheriff. If you had not come along—"

Rankin was looking down the alley after Sam. He had overheard Sam mention Ben; obviously there was some connection between them. He felt disturbed and angry; things were getting out of hand.

"Two of them in one day," Toreno muttered, as though reading his thoughts. In a grieved tone: "Both of them askin' about a horse I have not seen . . . a man I do not know."

Rankin turned sharply on him, his lips curling. "You're a liar!" he said coldly. "But it's your lie, and you'll have to stand behind it when they come back!"

Toreno just looked at him. Rankin turned and walked away. Toreno waited until the sheriff had gone; then the long-suffering look vanished from his face.

"Let them!" he whispered. "Let them come back. Maybe they will find the piebald horse they are lookin' for." His laughter had a sudden edge.

"But the Sonora Kid they will never find!"

CHAPTER SEVEN

— No Peace in Padre Valley —

The Cambriano acres reached from the confluence of the Aztec and the Bronco Apache River along a fertile stretch of bottomland to the arid hills twenty-three miles north. Actually the old Cambriano land grant had included all of Padre Valley and some twenty thousand acres south of the Rio Grande. But Don Cambriano, a wise and tolerant man, had not brought civil suit when Mexico had refused to recognize his claim to the land south of the river. Nor had the good Don exercised his rights concerning ownership throughout Padre Valley. He was content with the vast acreage still under his direct control; content to raise cattle for a living and horses as a hobby. He spent by far more time and money on his horses, blooded stock mostly, imported from Spain.

His house was old. It had been built by Alphonso Juan y Cambriano more than a hundred years before. It had the patina of age and the reflection of a hundred years of gracious living. The hacienda had formality to its grounds, and beauty, for women had always been an integral part of it. There were flower gardens and grape arbors and vegetable patches, all watered by an intricate system of *acequias* murmuring softly in the summer heat.

It was a two-hour ride from Avalon to the hacienda hidden from town by a spur of the low sand hills. An excited youngster had announced their coming before they rode under the adobe archway into the big yard, and a portly Mexican woman and a wiry, humorous-eyed man of sixty came out of the main house to greet them.

The portly woman Julia called Maria, and Ben gathered she was like a mother as well as housekeeper for the Cambriano children. The wiry man was her husband. Maria welcomed them with fussy warmness while her husband called to one of the men working in the stables to take care of the horses.

Don Cambriano was seated in a chair on the wide veranda that looked over the broad river bottomland. He had his head back against the cushion between him and the wall, and his eyes were closed. A blanket was tucked in around his legs and lower body.

He turned his head as Julia and Carlos, accompanied by Ben Craig, approached his chair. Ben saw that the *haciendado* was a small, portly man with crinkles of good humor around his dark eyes, a small gray mustache under a thin, aquiline nose. His face, though, was pale, almost waxen, as though he had been ill.

Don Cambriano's eyes widened in surprise as he saw them. "Carlos! I'm glad you came home! Did you get my letter?"

Carlos nodded. "I returned as soon as I got word," he answered. He bent and embraced his father. "I understand you have been hurt?"

"A gunshot wound in my leg," the older man replied. His voice sounded tired. "I'm afraid, Carlos, that it is age as much as the wound that is wearying me. I am glad you have come home. I want you to remain here now. Enough of schooling, eh, Carlos?"

The young Cambriano nodded. "There is indeed much to do, Father," he murmured. He turned then and made a gesture to Ben. "This is Ben Craig. I have invited him to stay with us, Father."

Don Cambriano's eyes showed perplexity. But he nodded in welcome and held out his hand to Ben. "I'm pleased you have honored us, *Senor* Craig."

Beside the Wells Fargo agent Julia was taking off her hat. She loosened her hair, and Ben noticed it was auburn and had a natural wave. She was chatting with the buxom housekeeper in an uninhibited manner that hinted either at loose parental restraint or at an understanding quite at variance with the strict customs usually ruling women of Spanish upbringing.

She turned to her father. "Perhaps you can help *Senor* Craig, Father," she said. "He has come here looking for—" she turned to Ben with slightly embarrassed smile—"gosh, Ben, I have forgotten the name."

It sounded odd and yet somehow pleasing to hear the girl say, "gosh," and Ben felt a sudden affinity for this tall, well-shaped daughter of Don Cambriano with the touch of red gold in her hair.

"The Sonora Kid," he supplied, smiling.

The old Don frowned. "A friend, *Senor* Craig?"

The Wells Fargo man shook his head. He saw no reason to keep his identity a secret. In fact, he was certain that Don Cambriano's reticence was due to a well-founded suspicion of all "gringo" strangers riding into Padre Valley.

"I'm a Wells Fargo special agent," he said bluntly. He reached inside his pocket for his wallet and showed them his identification. "The man I'm after dynamited a train, killed three men and stole ninety thousand dollars from the baggage car . . . money being transported from the Wells Fargo back in Denver."

Don Cambriano's eyes widened. "You have followed him here to Padre Valley, *Senor* Craig?"

Ben nodded. "He rode into Avalon last night.

That much I know. He may have left, making a run for the Border on a fresh horse, but—" Ben looked at Julia and Carlos—"I have a hunch he's still here, in Avalon."

Carlos met Ben's gaze; he smiled. "Avalon has become a refuge for many of his kind . . . men fleeing from the law up north. But if he has that much money with him, my hunch is that he's gone."

"Perhaps," Ben said. "But I understand there's a band of *revolucionistas* camped just across the Line, a few miles out of Saludad. The Sonora Kid would know this . . . and the risk involved if he were picked up with that money in his saddlebags."

"You are right, *Senor* Craig," Don Cambriano agreed. "He may well be still in Avalon . . . and I suggest you look for him in a cantina called The Maverick's Hangout."

"I have heard of the place," Ben admitted.

Julia was standing, pulling her left glove off her fingers. . . . She seemed lost in thought. Now she roused, looked at Ben. "Now I remember you, Ben," she said. "The name was mentioned in the home of friends, in Austin." She smiled. "I was inclined to take their stories with—shall we say a grain of salt? But I, too, have become an admirer. Few men would have dared to handle *El Rojo* so unceremoniously as you did this afternoon."

At both her father's and Carlos' inquiring glance, she explained the incident of their meeting on the road to Avalon.

The old Don's eyes were grateful as he looked up at Ben. "I am indeed honored to have you in my house, *Senor* Craig."

Ben shifted uncomfortably. "There is another reason I feel the Sonora Kid is still in Avalon," he said, trying to change the subject. "He must be familiar with Padre Valley, for no stranger would so quickly have found the goat trail leading down the face of the Tenido Barrier."

Don Cambriano's face was a study. "I myself did not know of any such trail," he confessed. "That there is one, I have heard rumors. But as beyond the Barrier there is only desert—" He shrugged. "I can understand why you think this outlaw belongs here."

Julia was staring at Ben, her eyes bright with interest. "This Sonora Kid, Ben," she asked, "what does he look like?"

"I have no good description of him," Ben answered; "only that he is a cold-blooded killer, a very clever holdup man. He is young and slender, and holding up trains seems to be his specialty. Sometimes he raids alone; other times he has a Mexican partner. On this last job the engineer thinks that he was hit in the face with a bullet . . . a grazing shot, possibly, for it did not stop the Kid. Still, it would leave some sort of scar."

Carlos grinned broadly. "What bad luck, Ben! I have such a scar." He brushed the scab under his left eye. "Only it happens that a quite jealous *senorita's* fingernails . . ." He shrugged, leaving the rest to be inferred.

His father was frowning. "Killers are everywhere in Padre Valley now, Ben. The Sonora Kid may easily be one of those who rendezvous at The Maverick's Hangout." He bit his lips. "Padre Valley was at peace for nearly one hundred years. And now trouble is everywhere. Across the Rio, as you have mentioned, a ragged peon named Chico Montero has gathered around him an equally ragged army who call themselves 'liberators.' Not that many of their grievances are not just ones. But I am afraid that under the banner of 'liberty and equality for the poor,' they are more interested in robbing and pillaging their fellow sufferers.

"Here—" he shook his head sadly—"it was unfortunate that the first Americans to come into Padre Valley were men fleeing from the law. We are remote here, far from Texas justice. Pablo, our local *jefe*, seldom had more to do than to escort a drunk or two to jail, or to fine a man for beating his wife. Now," the Don's voice turned bitter, "Pablo sulks in his home, jeered at by our people. I myself have been berated, insulted. And last week—" he rested his hand on his left thigh—"last week while riding in the foothills south of here, I was shot. My *vaqueros* are good men. But they are no match for the type of killer who has trained himself to use a gun as handily as my men use a branding iron or a riata. My herds are being depleted, my prize horses stolen—"

"In town there is a man who wears a sheriff's badge," Ben reminded the bitter man in the chair.

"The *Senor* Rankin?" Don Cambriano's voice was cold. "No one elected him to office, *Senor* Craig. He came to town one day, moved into Pablo's office, came out with a star on his coat. So it was described to me. Later, his deputy, Jesse Kane, showed up. Between them they keep order in Avalon, something Pablo could no longer manage. But he does not extend himself further. He seems to be waiting here . . . waiting for someone or something."

Carlos' voice held a deadly scorn. "He's like the others who have come to our land, taking over, as though they had a right to what is ours—what has been ours for generations—"

His father's hand checked his outburst. "No, no, Carlos. We have our grievances. But we must not condemn all for the misdeeds of the few." He laid his head back against the pillow, suddenly tired.

Julia came back to join them. She had changed into a fawn-colored skirt and a white blouse and she was carrying a tray with lemonade and glasses. “Something cool and refreshing—for hot tempers,” she said sweetly, looking at Carlos.

Her brother gave her a black look. Don Cambriano roused himself. “Perhaps *Senor* Craig would prefer some port,” he suggested.

“Lemonade will do nicely, after the ride from town,” Ben said. He reached inside his pocket for the makings, and his finger came in contact with the metal object the old soothsayer had given him in the plaza. He brought it out, eyeing it with sudden curiosity.

It was a brass coin about the size of a quarter, with the head of a bull stamped on one side and the small replica of Cortez on horseback on the other.

Carlos and Julia were eyeing it with restrained curiosity. He held it out for them. “I had almost forgotten,” he said, “but this is my reminder of an appointment with the Sonora Kid.” He told them of the incident in the plaza.

Julia shook her head. “It hardly makes sense. How would anyone know whom you were after—?”

“It’s true the Kid wasn’t mentioned by name,” Ben said, frowning. “But it is evident someone knows I am on his trail.” He shrugged. “It’s the only lead I have, now that the piebald horse I tracked all the way from Boxwood City has disappeared."

"Perhaps it is no more than a joke," Carlos intervened. "I know Jacinto who owns the *Corrida de Toros* well. He has strange ideas sometimes about attracting business."

His father waved his hand in sharp dismissal. "The *Senor* Craig is quite capable of taking care of himself, I'm sure, Carlos. In any event," he added firmly, "you will honor us by staying for dinner?"

Ben smiled. "I'm the one who is honored, Don Jose. But I have come a long way and I'm afraid I am not quite presentable." He rubbed the bristle on his chin with the back of his hand.

"A matter easily taken care of," the old Don said kindly. "Carlos, show *Senor* Craig to his room and have Melio arrange for whatever he needs."

Julia said swiftly, "I'll show him to his room, Father." She took Ben's arm before the old Don could answer and walked with Ben into the house.

They traveled down a long cool hallway, stopping before a closed door. "Ben," the girl said, "if you should find this Sonora Kid, what would you do?" She paused, her eyes dark and uncertain. "I know it sounds like a silly question—but I must know."

Ben regarded her with a slight frown. "I'm afraid the Kid will give me little choice," he said quietly.

"You mean—?"

"I may have to kill him," the Wells Fargo man answered. He tried to fathom the look he saw deep in her eyes. "Why are you concerned, Julia? You said you did not know this man."

Her lips trembled. "That coin, Ben. I think—" She put her hand on his arm, her voice troubled. "Please be careful tonight. I have a feeling that this appointment you have is no joke, despite what Carlos says. The *Corrida* has no good reputation in Avalon."

Ben nodded. "I'll keep my eyes open," he promised.

CHAPTER EIGHT

— Appointment with Death —

The stars over Padre Valley hung so low Ben Craig felt he could reach up and snuff them out, one by one. His buckskin moved along at an easy, ground-covering gait, and the Wells Fargo man let his thoughts slip back to the girl he had just left.

Julia Cambriano, he was now sure, knew who the Sonora Kid was. And the knowledge had frightened her.

Was it because the Kid was someone close to her?

Ben ran through his mind what he had learned that afternoon. Despite his tolerant attitude, Don Jose was growing bitter over the increasing depradations of his herds and the flouting of his authority which had until recently been absolute in the valley.

Carlos was obviously a hot-headed, rebellious youngster who shared his father's bitterness over the turn of events in the valley. He hated "gringos" and he hated Arch Rankin and he thought politically in terms of Mexico, rather than Texas. This was probably not unusual,

Ben reflected, since Carlos had been going to the University in Mexico City. If Carlos did not know the Sonora Kid, Ben concluded, the Kid at least had his sympathies.

While Don Jose had been too proud to come out openly and ask for Ben's help against the Maverick gang, the Wells Fargo agent knew the *haciendado* needed help. He would do what he could for Don Jose, but his main concern was still the Sonora Kid—and even as he decided this Ben Craig knew that the Kid was somehow tied to all the trouble here.

He thought of the coin in his pocket, and a tight, cold grin lifted the corners of his mouth. If the Kid had planned a trap, he would be in for a surprise.

Avalon loomed up in the night, a spatter of lights against the inky blackness. The Wells Fargo man came in from the west, hit San Pablo Avenue and turned the big buckskin toward the plaza. Ahead of him, blotting out the stars, loomed the bulk of San Pablo Mission, a testimony to the iron will of the Spanish missionary priests who had carried the word of God and the Cross into a heathen land.

The soft strains of a guitar tinkled on the warm night—a man's voice sang a Spanish song of love and death. And for an unguarded moment the tall Wells Fargo agent felt the prod of loneliness. Then he straightened in the saddle.

Ben's past was woven from the threads of a thousand lonely nights; his future out of the pattern of duty. He had shaped his life that way, and if occasionally he felt the stir of loneliness, it was because he was human. But Ben had long ago ceased to have regrets. Some men needed a woman and a home . . . an anchor holding them to one town, a way of life. Ben was not that kind of man.

He came out to the plaza, riding past the stone statue of Cortez to pull up at the rail at the south side of the plaza. His gaze held briefly on the slack-hipped pony farther down; a small smile touched his lips. He swung out of the saddle, dropped his reins over the tiebar, and was turning up the walk, toward the lighted windows of the *Corrida de Toros,* when Sam Jelco said: "Buy you a drink, Ben?"

Ben turned. Sam came toward him, out of the shadows where he had watched the Wells Fargo man ride in. He moved easily, his manner friendly. "Owe you somethin' for takin' those Apaches off my neck."

Ben hesitated. He didn't want Sam with him when he went into the *Corrida.* If the tip he had received from the old soothsayer was valid, he didn't want Sam Jelco in on it. If it turned out to be a trap, Sam would only be in the way.

He shrugged. "Never drink during business hours, Sam. Thanks, anyway."

Sam eyed him with a narrow-eyed grin. "Goin' somewhere?"

Ben nodded. Then, coldly: "The Sonora Kid could be across the Border, Sam."

Sam shook his head. "He could be . . . but he ain't." As Ben stared hard at him: "He took the shoes off his piebald, but he didn't fool me, either. I followed him to that stable back there," jerking a thumb in the direction of Toreno's place, "and I got the same answers from that fat Mexican you did. But you know, and I know, that the Kid's still in Avalon!"

Ben said: "There's a place in town called The Maverick's Hangout. He could be staying there."

Sam's grin was wide, jeering. "I've heard of the place. But that's not where you're goin', is it, Ben?"

Ben's voice went harsh. "Where I go is my business, Sam! Stay out of my way!"

He pushed past the bounty hunter, moving down under the arcade toward the *Corrida.* Sam looked after him, his grin turning to a sneer.

"Yore business, an' mine, Ben!" he said softly. "I'll let you find the Kid for me!"

The chunky Yaqui peon who had ridden the stage into Avalon with Julia Cambriano was at the *Corrida* bar when Ben Craig entered. He was nursing a glass of Mexican beer, his dusty serape across his powerful shoulders. His eyes caught Ben's reflection in the smoky mirror and an alert glitter came into his small black eyes. He picked up his glass and drifted across the narrow room to an unoccupied table near a door and sat down, leaning back against the wall, his big hat pushed down over his forehead.

Ben slowly crossed the room to the short, crowded bar. The air was full of *cigarillo* smoke and loud, excited Mexican voices. The pungent odor of spilled sour red wine mingled with the stronger smell of frying chile.

The *Corrida* was a busy place, and crowded, which was not surprising, for the dimensions of the cantina were small. There was a garden area in back, illuminated by flaring oil torches and set with small tables and benches discreetly placed under pineapple palms. This was reserved for those *caballeros* who brought their ladies. There was a private garden entrance in the high adobe wall which enclosed the area.

There was no visible entrance to the garden from the bar side, and Ben, glancing around, felt the weight of eyes on him. Americans who came to Avalon usually did their drinking at The Maverick's Hangout. . . . Here he stood out, a stranger and not entirely welcome.

Jacinto, the one-eyed cantina owner, was sweating at the far end of the bar. He gave Ben a cursory glance, then stiffened slightly. His gaze swung sharply to the chunky Yaqui peon, who had crossed to the small table by the door near the kitchen. The man seemed asleep, his chair tilted back against the adobe wall, his hat way down over his face.

Jacinto finished drawing his last glass of beer, sliding the loaded tray across to a small, limping Mexican waiter who carried it to his customers. Then, wiping his hands carefully on his towel, Jacinto crossed to Ben.

"Beer, *senor*?"

Ben nodded. He watched Jacinto draw his glass, set it in front of him. Then he drew out the small coin the fortuneteller had given him in the plaza and pushed it toward Jacinto.

The cantina owner reacted sharply. His big palm slapped down over it. . . . He glanced again toward the table near the kitchen door, and his lips tightened harshly. The chunky peon was gone!

He pushed the coin back to Ben. "You have made a mistake, *senor.* Ten *centavos*, please?"

Ben studied his face. Something had frightened the big man. . . .

"I was told it was a valuable coin," Ben said evenly, "worth much more to you than a glass of beer."

"You were misinformed," Jacinto said hurriedly. He glanced again toward the door near the kitchen. Tiny beads of sweat gleamed on his forehead.

He shoved the coin into Ben's hand. "The beer is on the house, *senor.* But I strongly advise that you drink it and leave!"

Ben slid the coin into his pocket. He took out a quarter and tossed it on the counter.

"Thanks for the advice," he said coldly. He turned, crossed the room to the door near the kitchen and went inside.

Jacinto stared after him, his heavy jowls quivering with apprehension. Then he quickly removed his towel, tossing it under the bar; he turned and ducked into the kitchen, crossing past a fat Mexican cook and her boy helper, neither of whom gave him a glance. He was about to step outside when a powerful hand thrust itself in front of him, bringing him up short.

The Yaqui peon was a thick shadow in the doorway. He said in a quiet, guttural command: "Go back inside, Jacinto!"

Jacinto stared across the garden area to the Mexican moving quickly back into the thick shadow of a pineapple palm. The man wore a bandolier across his chest; he carried a carbine in his hands.

The torch flare made the night shadows dance in the garden. . . . The tables were untenanted, the benches empty. Tonight Jacinto had closed the garden area, reserving it for a meeting he had planned for someone else.

The Yaqui peon's voice carried a growling menace. "*Vamos*!" Jacinto felt the prick of a knife through the shirt clinging to his ribs; wordlessly, he turned and went back into the kitchen.

The side door carried Ben out into a narrow alley which ran alongside a high adobe wall behind the *Corrida.* He followed it for fifty yards, coming to a small, wrought-iron gate usually fastened by a chain and padlock. But the chain hung loose now and the gate was slightly ajar. Ben pushed it inward and went inside, stooping to clear the first branches of a magnolia tree. The scent of its blooms hung heavy in the night air, clean and sweet after the kitchen odors inside the cantina.

It was quiet in the garden. The voices from inside the *Corrida* filtered through the thick adobe walls, muted and softened. Ben moved toward the nearest table, his gaze searching the shadows. He moved like a cat, alert and watchful. . . . He sensed someone in the garden and stopped, the torchlight flickering across his hard face.

A step at the garden gate swung him around: a woman's voice called quickly: "Ben!"

And then, out of the corner of his eye, he

caught the glint of light on a rifle muzzle. He jerked back and around, his hand leaping to his holstered gun. . . .

The Mexican *bandido* in the shadows of the palm fired once, his bullet screaming past Ben's head. Ben's bullet tore into him, spinning him around, smashing him back against the adobe wall.

Ben crouched, waiting . . . *it had been a trap after all!* His gaze swung to the girl standing frozen by the iron gate. Her voice held a note of suppressed hysteria: "Ben!"

He started to move toward her, twisted violently as her voice tore sharply at him in sudden warning: "Ben! Look out!"

The knife missed him by inches, making a rustling sound in the hibiscus beyond him. Ben whirled, caught a glimpse of a thick shadow by the *Corrida* kitchen door. He fired twice, his bullets smashing into the adobe around the framing. But the man who had thrown the knife was gone.

He started for the door, but stopped, thinking better of it. The knife-thrower would be lost in the crowd by the time he got there, and he knew he would receive no help from Jacinto's customers.

He turned and crossed quickly to the man he had killed. The bandolier, the ragged clothing, the wiry hardness of body indicated he was one of the *revolucionistas* from across the Border. But what he was doing there, in Avalon, and why he had been set up to ambush him escaped Ben.

"Ben! Please come away . . . quickly!"

Ben turned to face Julia Cambriano. She made a quick motion toward the gate. "It is dangerous here!"

He nodded and went over to her. Together they left the garden, moved quickly down the alley. As they came out to the plaza a tall shadow loomed up, blocking their passage.

The girl gasped. Ben shoved her aside, brought up his gun and held it cold and steady as he glimpsed the badge on the man's coat.

Rankin's voice was bleak. "Trouble, Mr. Craig?"

"Nothing I can't handle," Ben answered evenly. He eyed Rankin coldly. "You seem to have a habit of appearing right after it happens, Sheriff!"

"You judging . . . or condemning?" Rankin's voice held a bitter edge.

"Take it any way you like!" Ben snapped.

"Arch," Julia cut in quickly, "he is a friend, not an enemy. There is no need—"

"What are you doing here, Julia?" Rankin interrupted. His voice was stiff. "I thought you had gone home."

"I came to warn Ben . . . to tell him to stay

away from the *Corrida's* garden." She moved up between them. "I had the feeling there would be trouble—"

Ben looked sharply at her; she avoided his gaze, her attention on Rankin. She could have warned him back at the hacienda, Ben reflected coldly. Why had she waited until he rode into town?

"Arch, Ben is looking for the Sonora Kid!" Her voice was quick; there seemed to be some meaning in her statement that was reserved only for Rankin and herself.

Rankin frowned, turning his attention to Ben. "What happened back there?"

Ben was in no mood to answer civilly. "Why don't you go and find out?" he said harshly.

"I will!" Rankin snapped. He turned to the girl. "Julia, wait for me in the office. I'll ride you home!"

The girl nodded. She turned to Ben, stiffening slightly as Ben said flatly: "Who is the Sonora Kid?"

She hesitated briefly; then: "I don't know, Ben. Not for sure."

"But you've got a pretty good idea, haven't you?"

Julia shook her head. "It isn't enough, Ben." She put a hand on his arm. "Is it worth your life to find out?"

Ben looked at her. "Whose life, Julia? Mine . . . or his?"

She had no answer to that. She turned quickly and started across the plaza toward the sheriff's office. Ben looked after her for a moment, turning when Rankin said with bitter hostility:

"Keep away from her, Ben!"

Ben shrugged. "She followed me here, Sheriff . . . not the other way around."

Rankin stiffened. "Just you keep away from her!"

"Why?"

Rankin took a moment to reply. Then his voice softened, but the deadliness in it was unmistakable. "I've run into your kind before, Ben . . . if that's your name! She deserves better!"

"Something like you?" Ben asked thinly.

Rankin chose not to answer that. He jabbed a finger in Ben's direction for emphasis. "I know what you came to town for, mister . . . you and your partner. . . ."

"Sam?" Ben's voice held amusement.

"He was two hours behind you, but he told the same story about looking for the Sonora Kid." Rankin's voice held a bleak warning. "The stage to Saludad leaves at eight in the morning. You can be on it, or you can ride north, out of Padre Valley." His voice harshened. "As long as you both are out of here by noon tomorrow!"

He didn't wait for Ben's answer. He strode past him into the alley, turning to the gate in the adobe wall. . . .

• • •

Ben walked slowly back to his horse. Sam Jelco was waiting for him, leaning against the tierack, a crooked Mexican cheroot between his lips. He grinned as Ben approached.

"Hi, partner!" he greeted Ben.

Ben looked coldly at him.

"Reckon you got the sheriff's back up," Sam continued. He turned his gaze across the plaza to the sheriff's office. "Who's the girl?"

Ben ignored him. He walked to his horse and started to tighten the cinch strap. Sam edged closer, still grinning, his teeth clamped on his cheroot.

"I've done a little snoopin' on my own, Ben," he said. "The Sonora Kid's in town all right . . . hidin' out." As Ben started to mount, Sam placed his hand on Ben's saddle. "I don't have yore scruples, Ben. I'm not worried who I hurt." He smiled knowingly as Ben looked down at him.

"The Kid's got friends here . . . that's why he came to Avalon. Friends like—" He turned to look meaningly toward the sheriff's office.

"Don't believe everything you hear," Ben said grimly. He swung his horse away from the rack, cutting across the plaza toward the law office. He wanted to talk to Julia, and the blazes with Rankin!

The rider coming in from the west intercepted him just beyond the statue of Cortez. Carlos leaned forward over his saddle horn, his dark eyes surveying Ben, smothering the sharp surprise that momentarily gripped him.

"Ben—have you seen Julia?"

Ben looked at him, not answering immediately. This man had saved his life. And he was Don Cambriano's son! He did not need money. And yet—?

He indicated the law office. "She's inside, waiting for the sheriff. He promised to ride home with her."

Carlos' voice expressed displeasure. "The *Senor* Rankin is not welcome in my father's house," he said coldly. "I have come to take her back home."

Ben shrugged.

"And you—" Carlos asked—"will you come back with us?"

Ben shook his head. "Thanks, Carlos, but I think I'll stay in town tonight."

Carlos studied him. "You expect to find the Sonora Kid in Avalon?" he asked softly.

Ben smiled coldly. "Before morning," he said, "I will find him."

Carlos took a long slow breath. His smile matched Ben's. "I wish you luck, Ben," he said.

CHAPTER NINE

— "The Rendezvous is Tonight!" —

Arch Rankin straightened slowly from beside the body of the *bandido* and looked at Jacinto. The cantina owner was in the garden, along with a half-dozen men, customers more curious than those who discreetly remained behind. On the edge of this group the Yaqui peon stood silent, a stolid, indifferent spectator.

"I do not know how he got in here," Jacinto repeated, indicating the dead man, "or why."

Rankin eyed him coldly. The man was a liar, but he knew he would get nothing out of him. Not now . . . not at this time.

"One of Chico Montero's *revolucionistas*," Rankin said. "And you do not know why he was here?" His lips curled. "It could not be to meet a man . . . someone who might be willing to sell guns . . . brand-new Winchester repeating rifles . . . to the 'army of liberation' just across the Border?"

Jacinto shrugged. "I do not know who he is," he denied sullenly. "And I know of no meeting such as you describe."

Rankin ran his gaze over that small group.

Some of them were sympathizers, if not active followers, of Chico Montero. Misguided fools, he thought bleakly, trapped by impassioned catchwords. . . . They could not see that Chico Montero cared little for the downtrodden of Mexico. It was power Montero was after . . . and a thousand rifles would provide him with the sword to slash his way to that power.

Rankin made a gesture toward the dead man. "You will see that he is taken care of?" he asked Jacinto.

The big man nodded. "This trouble," he muttered, "it is not good for business."

Rankin's lips twisted coldly. "A dead man, Jacinto, is never good for business."

He turned and left the group, leaving by the abode wall gate. It would take him almost four hours to make the round trip to the Cambriano hacienda; he had the vague feeling that what he had been waiting for would happen tonight. It was in the wind, an ominous sense of tension. . . . Yet he had promised Julia he would see her home.

He crossed the plaza to his office, a small, hole-in-the-wall place entirely inadequate to the new demands of his job. Behind the desk was a tiny cell, accommodating not more than one prisoner at a time. It had been used sparingly by Pablo. Rankin had avoided using it at all.

He came into the office, his gaze searching

for Julia. . . . He reacted with surprise as he saw the short, round Mexican in his chair.

"She left not more than a minute or two ago," the man said, "with her brother, Carlos." He watched Rankin walk slowly to the wall to hang his hat on a hook. "She said to tell you she couldn't wait."

Rankin's mouth turned slightly bitter. He turned to the man in the chair, shrugging. "You shouldn't be seen here, Pablo."

Pablo, the former *jefe*, made a gesture with his hands. "No one saw me." He stood up, eyeing Rankin with shrewd, respectful appraisal. "Let me tell her, *Senor* Rankin; tell her why you are here in Avalon."

Rankin shook his head. "Not yet, Pablo."

"Later it may be too late," Pablo said. He took a long breath. "For me, too, it is a strain."

Rankin smiled gratefully. "I know. It is hard to be laughed at. But you know there is no other way."

Pablo nodded. "Tonight, *Senor* Rankin. I have listened well." His lips tightened. "It will happen tonight. The man with the guns has arrived."

Rankin nodded, thinking of Ben Craig and his partner, Sam Jelco. This was the man Pablo meant, but somehow it did not square with some of the things that had happened.

"You better leave before Jesse gets back," he

told Pablo. "I would not want him to see you here."

Pablo crossed to the door, looked back at Rankin. "I do not trust him," he said simply. "There are too many traitors in Avalon tonight . . . too many who are not what they appear to be."

Rankin smiled. "One of them may even be Chico Montero, eh, Pablo?"

Pablo did not smile. "It is not impossible," he said gravely. "If the guns are here tonight, Chico Montero will be here, too." He hesitated for a moment; then: "You may need more help than I can give you, *Senor* Rankin."

Rankin shrugged. "Not if I stop the gun-runner before he delivers them," he said.

He walked to the door and watched Pablo leave, moving quickly into the thick shadows under the arcade. He waited there, more disturbed than he had let on to Pablo.

That afternoon his mission had seemed simple. Jesse Kane had definitely identified the newcomer as the man they both had been waiting for: Rick Stevens, soldier of fortune and gun-runner.

Rankin sighed. He still had moments when the past seemed more real than the present. The smells and the chatter that reached him from across the plaza were suddenly alien, and it seemed to him odd that he should be standing there, less than twenty miles from the Mexican Border, rubbing elbows with sudden death.

A dumpy woman, a black shawl pulled around her heavy shoulders, walked past the office, hauling a reluctant *muchacho* homeward. Their passing brushed against his awareness. But the voice he was listening to was out of his past: it belonged to his college roommate. Whiskey-thickened but precise, it was toasting him on the eve of their graduation.

"To Archy, our future poet laureate!"

Quite consciously Rankin slid his right hand over the familiar bone handle of his Colt. Wryly he recalled that he had written little poetry since leaving the University. A United States deputy marshal's needs ran along more practical lines.

Between Boston's Beacon Hill and Padre Valley was a distance measured in more than miles. But the path by which Rankin had arrived there was not as strange as it might seem. An uncle in the diplomatic service, a footlessness after graduation, and a visit to Washington . . . a curiosity aroused by talk and speculation as to the future of the giant State of Texas, beginning to recover from the effects of the Civil War.

A commission as a United States federal officer had been easy to come by . . . and the early years had been routine.

It must be some strange quirk within him, he

reflected, which had made him more interested in bringing law and order to that violent land than in other branches of federal employment, or in the business house his family ran in Sommerville.

He had done well as a law officer, he thought, or he would not have been selected for this assignment. Across the river Chico Montero and his ragged band were at the moment only a nuisance. But once they were armed with modern rifles, the picture would change overnight.

Word had come through to headquarters that a gun-runner named Rick Stevens and an arsenal of rifles, two field guns, Colts and ammunition had left St. Louis. Destination: Padre Valley. Delivery: Across the Border.

So Arch Rankin had come to Padre Valley. To Pablo he had shown his credentials, revealed his mission. To the rest of the valley he was just a hardcase from up north who had eased fat, ineffectual Pablo out of office and taken over. He had promptly set a pattern that indicated his badge of office was only a cover-up and that in truth his sympathies were with the hard-faced men who rode into Padre Valley with one eye on their back trail and a quick hand on their gun butts.

He had not guessed his job would become complicated by a swaggering young Mexican's unreasoning hatred, or that he would fall in love with the man's sister, Julia Cambriano!

Or that the gun-runner, Rick Stevens, would have a partner—

A shadow moving quickly across the patches of light in the plaza caught his attention and pulled him back to the moment. He recognized the balanced cat walk of the man before Jesse Kane loomed up in the light of the window and Rankin caught the hard brightness in the deputy's cat-yellow eyes.

Kane's right hand was bandaged, but he used it to jerk open the door and close it quickly behind him as Rankin followed him inside. He turned to the sheriff, his voice rasping impatiently.

"What are you going to do about him, Arch?" The insolence in his tone had been growing, Arch noticed. "You've been waiting for Rick for a long time. What are you going to do about him now?"

Rankin eyed the deputy with a cold regard. He had not liked Kane from the day the blond gunman had walked into his office and suggested Rankin needed a deputy. He had taken the man on because it fitted in with the role Rankin had wanted to create there and because this man obviously was one of the hard-eyed breed with a dark back trail.

One day he had mentioned Rick Stevens to

Kane, indicating he was waiting for the man to show up in the valley, wanted to see him for personal reasons. He had not expected to hit pay dirt, and so was surprised when Kane frowned. "Shore, I know Rick. Gun-runnin's his business. Didn't know he was headed this way, though."

And Kane had added, shrugging: "If you want to see him that bad, Arch, I'll let you know soon as he shows up."

Rankin thought of that now, trying to fit the tall man who called himself Ben Craig into the frame of Rick Stevens. A small matter annoyed him, and he said: "I want to make sure he's Rick Stevens, Jesse. You said you knew him. But he didn't seem to know you. And the way he handled you—"

"I didn't say we were friends!" Kane cut in harshly. His words were blurred when he talked fast, hampered by his swollen lips. Rankin's reference to the beating he had taken stung, and he jabbed back, his eyes mirroring the sneer his lips could not fashion.

"That big feller is Rick all right. And he works fast. Right away he gets on the right side of that cocky Mexican, Carlos, an' starts shinin' up to that greaser sis of his—"

He stopped talking, his breath sucking in between his battered lips. He had not seen Rankin move, but there was a gun in the tall man's hand and a pinched whiteness around Rankin's mouth that warned Kane he had just overstepped himself.

He said thickly: "I'm sorry, Arch! I forgot y'o're sweet on that girl—"

"Miss Cambriano to you!" Rankin's voice was strained. "You just keep remembering that, Jesse!"

The deputy took in a cautious breath. "Shore," he agreed. "I meant no offense. I reckon I ain't used to but one kind of woman—"

"We'll leave the discussion of women out of our conversation," Rankin interrupted harshly. "Confine yourself to business!"

Kane shrugged. "Came out of the doc's office a few minutes ago. Rick was just coming out of the Mission Restaurant. I watched him ride toward The Maverick's Hangout. Probably got friends waiting—"

Arch frowned. "You never mentioned Rick had a partner."

"Partner?" Kane was genuinely surprised.

Arch nodded. "Man named Sam Jelco." He eyed Kane coldly. "You know him?"

Kane nodded slowly. "Bounty hunter." He made a small gesture of irritation. "Didn't know Sam was in town." He turned slowly to face the window. "If Sam's in town there's gonna be trouble. But," he turned back to Rankin, "I promise you one thing, Arch. Sam ain't Rick's partner!"

Rankin joined him at the window. "Then what is he in Avalon for?"

Jesse's smile was twisted. "Someone with a price on his head . . . a big price, or Sam wouldn't have come this far south, Arch."

Rankin looked out into the night. He felt suddenly caught up in a tangle of events he had not counted on. He felt confused and ineffectual, and the bitterness showed in his eyes.

"I don't care who Sam is after," he said. "Rick will have to contact someone tonight . . . the man with the money to buy his guns. And that's who I'm after, Jesse!"

Jesse's face was turned away from Rankin's; the sheriff did not see the small, satisfied gleam in his eyes. . . .

CHAPTER TEN

— One Maverick Too Many —

Ben Craig emerged from the Mission Restaurant and stood for a moment by his buckskin horse, weighing his next move. Sam was somewhere around, watching him . . . waiting for him to move in on the Kid. Then the bounty hunter would try to move in, make his play. It wasn't Sam who bothered him . . . he could take care of himself with Jelco.

But Sheriff Rankin puzzled him. An obviously educated man, he didn't seem to belong in Padre Valley. The sheriff's star on his coat was a sham. He was either a man on the run from the law, or he was playing a game . . . and Ben was inclined to believe the latter.

Rankin's hostility toward him was not easily explained. From the moment they had met Rankin had been hostile; his attitude had not improved when he found out Ben and Julia had met. The man was in love with the girl, Ben reflected, but he had a strange way of showing it.

He mounted and swung the buckskin away from the rack. He had heard The Maverick's Hangout mentioned many times today . . . it was time he found out just what sort of a place it was. It was possible, he reflected grimly, he might even get a line on the Sonora Kid there. . . .

He rode slowly up the street, catching a glimpse of Jesse Kane out of the corner of his eye. The deputy was watching him ride by. Ben smiled coldly. Neither Kane nor Rankin was what he claimed to be . . . and again he felt that they were tied up with the Sonora Kid somehow; with the Kid's reasons for coming there, to Padre Valley, instead of making a run for the Border.

A medley of raucous voices flowed out into the street ahead of him, drawing Ben's narrow-eyed attention to the adobe saloon flaunting its insolent legend: THE MAVERICK'S HANGOUT.

Ben's glance slid carelessly over the half-dozen horses standing slack-hipped at the rack. Then his gaze steadied and he straightened abruptly, jerking the buckskin's head toward the crowded rail.

The piebald stood off at the far end of the line—a big, rangy animal with a deep powerful chest. It looked like the kind of cayuse that could have made the grueling run from Boxwood City.

Ben reined his horse alongside the piebald and slipped easily out of the saddle. The piebald turned a mean eye in his direction, but Ben gripped the animal's left hind leg with a quick, firm grasp, bringing it up between his legs like a blacksmith getting ready to hammer on a shoe. The piebald jerked at his reins and snorted angrily.

The light at the hitch rack was bad. Ben pressed his thighs against the piebald's leg, freeing his hands long enough to produce a match and scrape it on the iron shoe. The tiny flame lasted long enough for Ben to verify that there was a tiny crescent gouge between the frogs—a marking he had followed for more than seven hundred miles!

So the Cambrianos had been right after all, he thought grimly. The Sonora Kid was no stranger to Padre Valley; he belonged to the Maverick gang!

He dropped the piebald's leg, moved quickly aside and slapped the animal's flank. The Kid was pretty simple-minded, he reflected bleakly. He had taken off the piebald's shoes just long enough to throw his pursuers off his trail; then he had reshod the animal with the same shoes. It didn't make sense, and because it didn't a vague irritation nagged the Wells Fargo man.

He turned to the saloon, his hand sliding briefly over the butt of his Peacemaker. Then he pushed the slatted doors aside and paused just inside, stepping out of line with the doors to let his eyes accustom themselves to the lamplight.

The noise faded down to a murmur as men turned their attention to the newcomer. The Hangout was restricted territory and tacitly observed as such by the natives of Avalon. Only men who belonged to the common fraternity walked in, or strangers who had not yet learned who were welcome there.

Ben's glance ranged over the small, narrow room. There was a plain, varnished wood bar against the left wall; the back shelves were well stocked with liquor. A faro table was set against the rear wall, next to a rear door, and half a dozen card tables were scattered throughout the rest of the room. There were no windows other than the two small, dirty-paned ones fronting the street.

At least ten rough-looking customers were in the Hangout. Two were at the bar, not counting the one-armed, hollow-cheeked man who served them. One was a buck-toothed youngster with long yellow hair curling over his ears shaggy down his thin neck. He wore a single broad cartridge belt from which two tooled leather holsters hung snugged in tightly against his slim hips. Walnut butts reflected the lamplight. Narrow black pants were tucked into spike-heeled boots ornamented soley by a pair of grimly utilitarian "bronc spurs."

This was the only man the Wells Fargo special agent could place. Oklahoma! A fast gunhand who counted sixteen dead men—wanted by most authorities from the Canadian Border to Mexico. This was the gunman, not yet turned twenty-one, who was reputed to have caused Bat Masterson to back out of a gunfight!

The man siding the bar with him was in his mid-thirties. A slender man of handsome appearance, he was the only man in the room in town clothes. He wore a heavy gold watch chain looped across his gray waistcoat; the bulge of a shoulder holster showed unmistakably under his coat.

All eyes were fixed on Ben as he moved away from the wall, heading for the bar. The slender man was chewing on a thin cheroot, a neutral expression in his dark brown eyes. Oklahoma frowned slightly, his pale eyes watchful.

As Ben came up to the bar the sour-faced bartender asked: "What's yore choice, stranger?"

"Rye," Ben answered, lifting his right foot to the scuffed rail. A glass was set up in front of him. The bartender turned for a bottle.

Ben reached over and took the bottle standing in front of the yellow-haired gunslinger. "This brand will do," he said shortly. The bartender scowled, glancing at the slender man for his cue.

Oklahoma dropped his elbow from the counter

and swung around to face Ben. The man at his side put a hand on his elbow. The gunman took a quick breath and turned back to his drink.

Ben poured, lifting the glass to his lips. A black-striped gray cat with a badly chewed left ear jumped on the counter and came padding toward Ben as he set his glass down. The tom hooked out a paw and pulled Ben's glass toward him and started to lap up the rest of Ben's drink.

Ben eyed the alcoholic feline without expression. The bartender sneered: "That's Omar. Holds his likker better'n most men. Two to one he can drink you under the table, feller!"

The Wells Fargo man lifted his gaze to meet the bartender's. "Someone sure short-changed you when they passed out brains," he said disgustedly. He shoved Omar away, dumped what was left of the whiskey into the cuspidor at his feet. "Go mooch yore drinks somewhere else," he growled to the puzzled tomcat.

The man behind the cheroot looked Ben over slowly, his lips twisting coldly around the smoke. "You're big, feller," he conceded, "and you talk tough. You come in here looking for trouble?"

Ben's eyes seemed to look right through the man. "I generally move up to meet it," he admitted coldly.

Oklahoma stirred, pushed around to face Ben.

"You don't have to move far," he said flatly. "I don't like yore—"

The slender man cut him off sharply. "I'll handle this, Oklahoma!" He waited until the yellow-haired gunslinger turned reluctantly back to his drink. "I'm Cal Stetson," he told Ben. "Who are you?"

"I'm a man in a hurry," Ben answered bleakly. He had eliminated the two at the bar, and his glance now swung around to the other men in the saloon. "I tied up alongside a lame piebald," he said loudly. "Any man who'd leave his cayuse tied up outside like that while he killed the night playing cards ought to be booted out of town!"

At a table against the opposite wall a rangy man, whipped by sun and weather to leather toughness, pushed back his chair. "That piebald's mine!" he stated flatly. "And he wasn't lame when I left him out there!"

Ben Craig eased away from the bar. The rangy man's beard-stubbled features hid no recent bullet scar. His nose had been flattened across his face years before, and it was an old scar that traced its white gash under his chin.

This man was not the Sonora Kid! He was too big, anyway—and too old. But if he wasn't the Kid, he was riding the Kid's horse. And Ben wanted to know how he had come by the piebald.

"I trailed that piebald seven hundred miles!" Ben said harshly. "I want a good look at the murdering son who rode him!"

The rangy man looked annoyed. "Go look somewhere else," he said shortly. "I bought that piebald this morning. I haven't even been out of town with him."

"Who sold him to you?"

The man snorted angrily. "Cripes, Mike!" he called. "Throw this bum out, will you? I've got a pat hand here or I'd do it myself!"

Mike was sweeping around the faro table. He put his broom aside and came toward Ben, a heavy-shouldered ex pug with a battered face and vacant gray eyes. He shuffled up, extending a hairy, muscular arm. . . .

The Wells Fargo man wasted no time on the bouncer. He clamped a wristlock on the man, fell backward and flipped Mike across his hip. Mike landed on the poker table, skidding into the lap of the card player across from the rangy man. Both men wound up in a cursing tangle on the floor.

Ben faced the acknowledged owner of the piebald. "You just lost your pat hand," he growled. He reached out, hooked his fingers into the man's shirt front, jerked him up and across the table. "Who sold him to you?" he repeated. Ben's voice held a wicked impatience.

The rangy man jerked violently, tearing his

shirt as he lunged free. He got both hands under the table, jerked it up and into Ben and followed it, shoving his snarling companion aside in an effort to get at Ben.

He reached Ben first and almost immediately lost all interest in the ensuing melee. The big Wells Fargo agent's vicious right smashed his nose again. He fell across the path of the next man, who tripped and fell forward, arms flailing. His face collided with Ben's knees and he lost a perfectly good set of front teeth before ploughing his face into the rough board floor.

Mike followed him, shuffling more cautiously, his heavy jaw tucked in behind his right shoulder. He landed one blow high up on Ben's cheek before two solid smashes to the mid-section brought his arms down and a pained look to his eyes. A right cross sent him reeling across the crawling figure of the man who had lost his teeth. He fell on his back, hitting his head hard and lay there, blinking up at the ugly ceiling.

The other two card players landed several ineffectual punches. But they were half-hearted about the affair now, and Ben finished them off. He dropped the older, squint-eyed man with a hard left, whirled, took hold of the remaining man by the scruff of the neck and the seat of his pants and ran him across the room, ramming him head first into the bar front.

The scuffle had lasted less than a minute. It had started and ended with a grim abruptness that left the remaining men open-mouthed. In the momentary stillness Ben turned to the rangy man sitting on the floor, holding a handkerchief to his bleeding nose.

"We could have saved this for another time." Ben growled. "All I asked you was who sold you the piebald?"

"Toreno." The rangy man's voice was thick it his throat. "The Mexican stable man at the south end of town."

Ben took a slow breath. "Probably sold him cheap, too," he muttered. He bent to pick up his hat. From the bar Oklahoma's thin, reedy voice reached across the room. "Just a minute, big fella!"

Ben Craig straightened and turned slowly, reading the gunman's challenge in that cold order. Oklahoma had stepped away from Cal Stetson. He was standing over the unconscious figure of the man Ben had rammed against the bar, a scrawny-necked kid old before his time.

"Might be Lute was lyin' to you about that piebald," the yellow-haired gunslinger sneered. "Might be I sold Lute that cayuse. Might even be I'm the man you trailed into the valley!"

Ben's smile had an iron quality, hard and

assured. "You've been called a lot of things, Oklahoma," he said quietly, "but never the Sonora Kid."

The gunman's eyes flared with brief surprise. "You know me, eh?"

The room was still behind Ben, and he knew he had delayed too long. The others had recovered from their surprise and were waiting—waiting for Oklahoma to make his play!

He forced it, his voice brusque and cutting. "I know you—a two-bit gunman who should have had his toys taken away from him before he learned they could kill. I'm giving you a choice now. Use them—or get booted out of here!"

Ben Craig was standing in the middle of the quiet room when he issued the challenge; a long way from the front door. Oklahoma's hesitation was brief. He dropped both hands in a flashing, rolling draw, and he lived only long enough to retain a glimpse of a spurt of smoke wreathing the tall man's hip, rising up to hide a grim, dark face. Then the tearing pain in his chest spread a black veil across his pale eyes.

He was dead as he fell, but his tightening fingers sent two wild shots across the room just as Ben's gun blasted out the hanging lights!

In the blanketing darkness Stetson's angry

voice shouted directions: "Cover the doors! We'll get the blasted son before he can get away—"

He jerked violently, uttering a sharp curse as a bullet gouged into the bar front. Yells stabbed through the darkness. Several other shots flamed across the room, gouging splinters from the batwings.

Stetson yelled: "Hold it, you fools! Don't shoot until you see—" A steel-hard arm encircled his throat, choking off his orders. He was relieved of his shoulder gun, shoved violently toward the center of the room.

In the covering darkness Ben vaulted over the bar. He landed lightly and waited patiently. A man's quick, frightened breathing rasped in the momentary quiet, less than an arm's length away. Then the bartender's cautious voice whispered: "That you, Cal?"

Ben's grin was lost in the darkness. He reached out his left hand, touched a shiny bald knob and whispered: "Yeah, it's me," as he batted his Colt across the man's head. The bartender didn't even grunt.

Cal Stetson's wheezy voice broke the quiet. "He's still in here! Shoot at anyone going through those doors! Shorty, get that spare lamp from under the bar!"

Ben's hands closed silently around a pair of whiskey bottles on the back bar shelves. He heaved one in the direction of Stetson's voice, the other through the windows.

Jittery trigger fingers reacted spasmodically to the breaking glass. A half-dozen flames ripped the darkness as men shot at the sound of the smashing bottles. In quick succession Ben tossed three more, heaving the last one toward the batwings.

Gunfire raked the room. A man cried out in pain; another cursed violently. Ben dropped to his hands and knees and crawled swiftly to the far end of the counter just as the shots turned to the bar. In the ensuing fire the bar mirror was shattered, and most of the remaining whiskey bottles.

Cal Stetson's choked voice stopped the wholesale destruction. "We're wrecking the place! Wait until we see what we're shooting at!"

Ben was free of the bar. He remembered the small, pot-bellied stove by the side wall, its stovepipe elbowing halfway across the ceiling before it emerged through the flat roof.

A man's hoarse voice rasped impatiently: "Why doesn't Shorty come up with that light Cal?"

Ben reached the stove under cover of the man's voice. He rammed his shoulder against it, heaving it over. The long stovepipe came down in sections. The din was ear-shattering.

In the confusion the Wells Fargo man headed

for the door. He bumped into a cursing shadow, jammed the heel of his hand into the man's face, hit the batwings and was gone before the clamor of falling stovepipe had faded.

Five minutes later a wobbly-kneed bartender placed a spare lamp on the bullet-scarred counter and in the poor light surveyed the damage. The place was a shambles.

Cal Stetson swore wildly. "He got away!" His crushed larynx hurt him, made him wheeze out his words.

A stumpy man, wiping blood from his lips, shouldered through the batwings. His voice rose grimly. "He left his cayuse at the rack, Cal. He's still in town!"

Stetson headed outside, the others following. The big buckskin jerked at his reins, whistling a warning to the mean-eyed piebald next to him.

Lefty Grimes, a tall man with a cast in his right eye, said sharply, "I think I've seen that buckskin before, Cal. And I think I place the big feller now."

He ducked under the tierack and started to mount a sleepy roan.

Stetson snapped: "Where in blazes do you think you're going?"

Lefty's tone was curt. "The Border's twenty miles due south."

"You blamed fool!" Stetson raged. "The *rurales* are patrolling the river at Saludad!"

"I'll take my chances with the Mexican militia!" Lefty growled. He settled himself in the saddle. "That hombre who just left is Ben Craig, a Wells Fargo special agent."

Stetson stiffened. "You sure?"

Lefty shrugged. "He outgunned Oklahoma, didn't he?" He wheeled his roan away, heading at a quick canter up the street.

Stetson stared after him, speechless. The stumpy man who had been the first one outside looked back at the shambles inside the saloon. He gulped, grinning apologetically. "Reckon I feel like Lefty," he murmured. He climbed into the saddle of a long-legged dun horse and followed Lefty out of town.

Stetson's voice, still wheezy, held a sudden vicious intensity. "The next man who tries to leave gets a bullet between his shoulders!"

No one else moved.

CHAPTER ELEVEN

— The Deal —

Sheriff Rankin and his deputy, Kane, were standing by the law office when the first Colt shot boomed in the night, its muffled report indicating it had been fired indoors. Rankin tensed. The shot seemed to have come from the direction of The Maverick's Hangout.

A veritable volley of other shots followed almost immediately. Kane was frowning. "Sounds like a regular war, Arch. Coming from The Hangout, too." His eyes gleamed. "I wonder if—"

The shots quit abruptly. There was an interval of silence . . . then the jangle of bottles being smashed came to them. The gunfire ripped loose again, ended abruptly, and a man's faint yell rode the night.

"What the devil!" Kane muttered.

Rankin shook his head. "Sounds like a riot." He reached for his hat, checked his holstered gun and pulled the door open. He stepped off the walk into the plaza just as the falling stovepipe made a racket in the saloon on San Pablo Avenue.

Rankin broke into a run.

Jesse Kane tagged along as far as the statue of Cortez. Then he stopped, turning to face the dark hills just outside of town. He waited expectantly for the signal he knew was coming.

The one man riot was over by the time sheriff Rankin reached The Hangout. He had passed several small groups of spectators on the way, but no one had felt an urgent desire to investigate more closely the commotion in the saloon.

Rankin paused on the walk, turning to eye the animals at the rack in front of The Hangout. The big buckskin Rick Stevens had ridden into town was perking at his reins, trying to break loose.

So Stevens was the cause of the commotion inside The Hangout? Rankin had a mental picture of the tall man walking into the saloon for a drink and running into immediate trouble. The Maverick gang did not take kindly to outsiders.

A vague disappointment nagged at him as he put his hands up to part the batwings. He had wanted to take Rick Stevens alive. . . .

He pushed the doors open and stepped into a scene that brought him up short, eyebrows arching incredulously.

Two plain glass-based kerosene lamps were burning with a smoky light, one placed at each end of the bar. The light they cast was poor, but it was sufficient to show Rankin the devastation that had visited the outlaw hangout.

A pot-bellied stove lay overturned in a corner of the room. Sections of the stovepipe lay scattered among the debris of broken chairs and tables. The bar itself was riddled by more than a dozen .45 slugs. Shards of the long bar mirror still clung to the wall above shelves littered with fragments of bottles and still dripping whiskey.

The bartender was wearing a handkerchief knotted around his head. His eyes, moving to survey the sherff, had a sick-dog look. Cal Stetson was leaning wearily against the bar. He looked as though he had been roughly handled. At his feet lay the sprawled body of Oklahoma. Standing and sitting around the only table and several chairs remaining intact were a half dozen of Stetson's crew, most of them nursing an assortment of visible bruises and wounds.

Rankin took all this in with a quick survey, and the full impact didn't hit him at first. Where was the man Kane had said was Rick Stevens? His glance went over the room again, shifted back to Stetson's coffee-colored face. Stetson had a mean look in his eyes as he regarded the sheriff.

An unbelieving grin widened Rankin's mouth.

No man could have walked into The Maverick's Hangout, wreaked so much damage—and walked out again! And yet . . .

He stepped over sections of stovepipe and made his way to the bar. The atmosphere in The Hangout, he noticed with keen relish, besides being somewhat sooty, was definitely subdued.

Oklahoma lay curled on the floor, his two guns still gripped in his stiffening hands. Rankin stepped over the man's body and put his foot on the rail beside Stetson's. He leaned his lanky frame over the scarred counter, surveyed the mess behind the bar and turned to the outlaw boss, shaking his head slowly. "Looks like the wrath of the Lord visited you, Stetson," he said. His voice held no sympathy.

Stetson took a partially crumpled cheroot from his rumpled coat pocket and stuck it between his lips. "You're late getting here, Sheriff!" he wheezed.

Rankin's eyebrows went up a few more notches. "My, my, how your voice has changed, Mr. Stetson. I didn't realize you were so young—"

Stetson's face went ugly. "One joker is all I can stomach tonight, Sheriff! You looking for something in here?"

"For someone," Rankin amended, grave-faced. "I came looking for a gun-runner named

Rick Stevens. I expected to find him quite—shall we put it politely?—*hors de combat.*"

Stetson's eyes held a wary puzzlement. "Stevens? Why look for him in here?"

"His horse is still tied up at your rack," Rankin pointed out. "The big buckskin next to the piebald."

An unbelieving flicker passed through Stetson's eyes. "You mean the tall jasper with the thonged-down Peacemaker?"

Rankin nodded. "I'll give it to you straight," he said coldly. "I've been in town long enough to know your setup here in Padre Valley. You're seventy miles from the nearest Texas law and only twenty miles from the Mexican Border. If things ever got hot enough to bring Texas law down here, you could make it across the Line in a hurry. In the meantime you've been busy rustling Jose Cambriano blind.

"The only reason I've let you alone is because less than twenty miles from here a thousand hungry Mexican peons are just itching to get started on a little private war of their own. And they will not be too particular on which side of the Border they start shooting." Rankin's voice held little emotion; only a flat conviction. "Compared to them you're only a side issue, Stetson!"

Stetson sneered. "Chico Montero's gang wouldn't get within a mile of town before we'd cut them down. Most of his men don't have guns—"

"You're a fool!" Rankin snapped. "When Chico starts his little war he'll have guns; modern rifles for every man and ammunition to start his war!"

Stetson took this with a grain of salt. "Where would a dumb peon like Chico get a thousand rifles?"

Rankin sighed. He reached out and took Stetson's last cheroot and clamped his lips around it. "The man who just left here. I have good reason to believe he's Rick Stevens—the man with the guns for Chico Montero!"

Stetson smiled. It was a sudden grimace, like a cat who had spotted a mouse, and it brought a sudden rankling doubt to the sheriff.

"Why are you telling *me?*" Stetson asked bluntly.

Rankin hesitated. He had not expected to reveal this to the outlaw boss, and now, faced with the question, he gathered his reasons together, shaping them carefully.

"Because I might need your help," he said slowly. "And you'll need mine," he added tartly. "I'm offering you a deal, because right now I can see no other way to stop Montero. If Stevens gets those guns through to Chico—"

Stetson chewed on his unlighted cigar. He was suddenly agreeable. "I see your point,

Sheriff. A thousand armed greasers—" He shrugged. "What's the deal?"

"You help me stop Stevens," Arch said coldly, "and I'll give you and your men a chance to clear out of Padre Valley!"

Stetson's lips pursed. "That's not much of a deal, Sheriff. I could refuse—" His sudden smile denied this. "But I've got a personal score to settle with—ah, Stevens. You can count on me and my boys to help."

Rankin nodded. Something was wrong, but he couldn't pin it down. He asked casually: "What happened in here?"

Stetson chose his explanation. "This tall feller you say is Stevens walked in here looking for trouble. Wanted to know who owned the big piebald tied up at the rail. Lute bought the animal from Toreno . . . the Mexican who owns a livery stable on the edge of town." Stetson filled in the details, making the element of surprise strong, toning down Ben's part. He ended maliciously with: "I ain't admitting my men have been rustling Cambriano stock. But even if we were, it's downright honest compared to selling guns to a bunch of filthy peons across the Border. Any man who'd do that—"

The small doubt in Rankin's mind began to grow. Mentally he berated himself for the impulse that had led him to make a deal with Stetson.

But he had made the deal, and he would go through with it.

"I'll take Stevens' buckskin," he said. "Rick must still be in town somewhere. And he'll be wanting his horse." His eyes were bleak. "I want to be there when he comes for him."

Stetson nodded, his grin faintly derisive. "You better shoot fast, Sheriff—and make that first shot count." His gaze slanted to the body on the floor. He added grimly: "You won't get another chance!"

Rankin turned away, crossing the room to the door. Stetson leaned back against the bar and watched him go. Doubtful grins were on the faces of the men at the table. But there was no doubt in Stetson. He had just made one of the best deals of his life. He had been practically given a free hand to kill Ben Craig!

He turned to Shorty behind the bar. "If you can find one bottle left in that mess, bring it out. We've got a little celebrating to do. . . ."

Rankin paused in front of the tierack. A glow in the sky to the south caught the corner of his eye. He moved quickly down the walk until a break in the building line across the street gave him a view of the dark hills just outside of town.

He blinked. A small fire was burning on the slope of Santa Maria Hill; a peculiar fire. He stared, watching it brighten against the blackness. The heat of the day, still rising from the levels below, made the blaze shimmer—gave it dimensions that were deceiving. But Rankin would have taken an oath that the fire was shaped like a huge X.

It had flared up quickly, and already it was dying down. Santa Maria Hill. As nearly as he could judge, the fire was close to the small shrine of Saint Mary.

A signal fire? For whom?

He had a pretty accurate idea for whom the fire was intended and who had lighted it.

He turned back to the Maverick tiebar, feeling grim and sick at heart. He had kept making excuses, kept avoiding what his logical mind had already decided for him. But he couldn't avoid it any longer.

There was only one man in Padre Valley who had the money to pay for Chico Montero's guns!

The buckskin snorted as Rankin untied his reins and came alongside. "Easy, boy," Rankin muttered. "I won't hurt you."

He swung up into the saddle, and the buckskin pranced back into the street. Rankin patted the animal's arched neck. "You're too good a horse for the likes of him," he muttered.

He turned the animal toward the plaza, remembering that Kane had unaccountably remained behind. Had Kane seen the fire?

He rode past the statue of Cortez and pulled up before the law office. The lamp was still burning inside, its tiny glow making a splotch of light on the walk out front.

"Kane!" he called.

There was no stir from inside. Rankin frowned. He slid out of the saddle. "Wonder where he—"

The buckskin's snort warned him. But he had time only to turn full into the impact of a clubbed Colt. His knees sagged and he fell, only dimly aware of a dark figure stepping over him. He heard Ben's horse snort again, and then the gun blasted heavily in the night and lights exploded in his head. . . .

When he came to, a frightened Mexican was dabbing his head with a wet cloth. He had been dragged into the light from the office. Looking up, he recognized the old man as Juan, owner of the small tobacco shop three doors down.

He sat up. Juan said: "*Senor* Rankin, you must be quiet. I have sent my son for the doctor—"

"Where did he go?" Rankin rasped. "The man on the big buckskin horse? Which way did he ride, Juan?"

The old Mexican shrugged. "I did not see. When I came out you were lying here. I thought you were dead."

Rankin stood up. His knees felt wobbly. He lifted his hand to the side of his head and grimaced. The bullet had grazed him; the blood felt sticky on his probing fingers.

But a sense of urgency cut through his weakness. He had no doubt that it had been Rick Stevens who had been waiting for him. And now he was on his way to the shrine on Santa Maria Hill . . . to a rendezvous with the man who was to buy his guns!

Rankin's horse was in a shed behind the law office. He pushed Juan's hands away, ignoring the man's protests. He had waited five months for this to happen. He was hurt, and there was a sickness in the pit of his stomach. But he couldn't lie back now and let the whole thing slip through his fingers!

He turned and stumbled down the alley toward the shed. It would take him only a few minutes to saddle and ride out. He hoped bitterly that he would get to the shrine in time!

CHAPTER TWELVE

— "My Knife Is at Your Back!" —

Across the street from The Maverick's Hangout a broad, powerful figure detached himself from the darkness of a doorway and padded silently after Ben Craig's tall shadow. He had been headed up the avenue when he had seen the Wells Fargo man ride toward The Hangout, pull up at the rack and examine the piebald's hind shoe. So he had waited, a squat and silent figure, wrapped in his own patience.

He waited through the commotion and shooting that drew small clusters of spectators into wary groups along the street. Finally he saw Ben emerge and immediately identified the tall figure who turned quickly up the street, merging almost immediately into the shadows.

The squat Yaqui followed quickly, moving with the silent, deadly patience of an Indian.

Ben Craig prowled through the dark alleys, heading for Toreno's. His coat was ripped under his left arm and there was a livid bruise high up on his cheek. Blood stained the corner of his mouth. He moved grimly, and men melted away at his approach, sensing the danger in the man.

The appointment set up for him in the *Corrida de Toros* had been a ruse to get him off the track. The Sonora Kid had been in town all along, and he had no intention of making a run for the Border. He was tied up with Toreno, and perhaps with Chico Montero . . . and Ben knew where to get at the truth now.

His thoughts went back to his horse, tied to the saloon rail. Sorry, fella, he apologized mentally. But I'll be back for you in an hour.

It took him five minutes to find the narrow, manure-littered way to Toreno's place. This was where the Kid had come last night. Ben was certain of it now. The Kid had pried the shoes off his piebald and ridden into town and turned the animal over to the fat Mexican who had so guilelessly denied seeing the animal.

A hard grin touched Ben's lips. What had started out as a simple manhunt was developing angles, some of which, he reflected coldly, seemed to reach across the Mexican Border.

A door opened in the darkness ahead, and the Wells Fargo man pressed quickly against the blackness of the nearby building.

A yellow oblong of lamplight, partially blotted out by a thick figure, spilled into the trampled yard ahead. The glare came from within living quarters at the end of the long adobe stable building.

Toreno paused in the doorway. Evidently

the disturbance at The Hangout had drawn him outside, but his curiosity had waned before he reached the avenue. He was going back inside now, a fat, slow-moving man in baggy pants. He glanced back into the darkness of the alley, scratched his head and shuffled inside.

He left his door open to the warm night and sat down on his bunk, scratching absently among the thick growth of hair on his chest.

Ben eased away from the building wall. He made it to Toreno's doorway without the fat man hearing him. Ben's looming figure warned the Mexican too late. His startled glance rose to Ben, and his mouth gaped in surprise. Then he started to get up, twisting for the shotgun on the wall above him.

Ben's voice was a whiplash. "Not this time, Toreno!"

The Mexican hesitated. He turned, his mouth going sullen as Ben took a step inside.

"You startled me, amigo," he said, recovering his oily composure. "I thought some horse thief, perhaps—"

"Or perhaps the hombre who bought the piebald from you, eh?" Ben cut him off sharply. He loomed tall in the small room, towering over the heavy stable man. "I swallowed your story the first time," he muttered grimly. "But this time I want the truth. I want to know who rode that piebald into Avalon!"

Toreno licked his lips. "*Por Dios*," he protested, "I do not know what you seek, *senor.* I have seen no such *caballo* as you have described!"

"You're a liar!" Ben snapped. The Wells Fargo man's eyes held a flat, uncompromising deadliness. "The Sonora Kid rode that piebald horse to your place last night and told you to get rid of it for him. You did. Only you decided you could pick up some easy money, perhaps, and still do the Kid a good turn. So you sold the piebald to one of the Maverick gang, knowing I'd eventually run across the animal and think I had my man. Quite possibly you had it figured out that the Maverick boys would shoot first, when I started asking questions."

A faint glitter shone briefly in Toreno's black eyes. "You give me much credit, *senor*," he said softly. "More than I deserve—"

"That's all I'm giving you!" Ben growled. "Now I want the answer. I want to know who the Kid is?"

Toreno sneered. "Why not look behind you, *senor* . . . and find out!"

Ben tensed. He had heard nothing. Yet a sudden prickling at the back of his neck warned him, and then it was too late. A soft, guttural voice hissed in his ear: "My knife is at your back, *cabron*! One wrong move—"

Ben kicked backward. He felt his boot jar

against a solid body, and the recoil sent him plunging forward. He was off balance, heading for Toreno, and he tried to draw his Colt.

The fat Mexican stable man brought both hands down in a chopping blow that caught the Wells Fargo agent across the back of his neck and shoulders. Ben's knees hit the edge of the bunk and he fell across it, momentarily dazed. He saw Toreno move, and some savage instinct of survival enabled him to twist aside just as Toreno brought the heavy butt of his shotgun down in a vicious jab for his face. He had his Colt in his hand, and he tilted it and fired once. He knew, with bitter regret, that he had missed. Then Toreno swung again. . . .

Toreno straightened slowly from Ben's sprawled figure and carefully propped his shotgun against the wall. His left ear was oozing blood where Ben's bullet had nicked it.

The squat Yaqui who had come down the alley behind Ben walked to Toreno. "He is *malo hombre*," he muttered. It is well to get rid of him now!" He bent over Ben's unconscious figure, the blade of his knife glittering in the lamplight.

"No! No!" Toreno's hand closed over the other's thick wrist. "Not here, Chico! Not now!" He turned and took a long stride to the oil lamp and quickly blew it out.

A velvety darkness came into the small room, blotting out details. Chico Montero took a deep breath.

"A dead man makes no trouble!" he argued dispassionately. "And a knife makes no noise!"

Toreno was at the door, listening. The night had its small disturbances: the nearby wail of an awakened child, the stamping of horses in the stalls next door, the mutter of angry voices on a vagrant breeze. But nothing indicated that the shot had aroused someone's curiosity. Shots were common enough in Avalon these days, Toreno reflected.

He turned back to Chico Montero. The Mexican revolutionary leader ran his thumb lightly over the keen blade. "No one will hear," he insisted harshly.

Toreno shook his head. "You will spoil everything. Already someone might have recognized you!" He made a gesture of impatience. "You should have stayed in Mexico—"

"Bah!" the other growled. "I have grown tired of waiting; of empty promises! My men grow impatient, restless. Where are those guns you have promised?"

Toreno turned on the stolid-faced man. "You fool!" he whispered harshly. "Do you think things like this can be arranged just like that?" He snapped his fingers. "For years I have played nursemaid and teacher to Don Jose's whelp. He was a *muchacho* when I took him on my knee and told him stories of our great general, Santa Ana. I filled his ears with the glories of Mexico and the wrongs our country has suffered. I molded him, Chico—with my voice I made him into what he is today. It has taken years. But now all my labors are paying off—"

The Yaqui snorted. "*Si*—you have lived here, growing fat, while I lived like a beast in the hills, waiting for you to make good your promises!"

"They will be made good!" Toreno snapped. "A thousand American rifles, the very latest, and ammunition enough to waste!"

"Where are they?"

"Near at hand. Of that I am sure, Chico. Last night Carlos returned with the money to pay for them." Toreno shrugged. "Tonight he was to light the signal fire at the shrine of Santa Maria that will arrange a meeting with the man who has the guns. He told me this last night."

"This man, then," Chico growled, turning to Ben's unconscious figure, "who is he?"

"A lawman who followed Carlos into the valley." He frowned, suddenly uneasy at the remembrance of Sam Jelco. "There was another who came looking for Carlos . . . a bounty hunter." His voice hardened. "There is much money at stake, Chico. If he should get to Carlos first—"

"It is time we drove to meet with Carlos then," Chico growled. His hand tightened on his knife handle as he turned to Ben. "And all the better reason why I should kill this one now!"

Toreno gripped his brother's muscled shoulder. "No! I have my reasons, Chico. Help me take him into the stable before he stirs. We will tie him securely, and when Carlos gives us the signal we will take him with us!"

Chico hesitated. He was a stolid man, not as nimble-witted as his brother, and after a moment's reflection he gave in. They took Ben out to the stable and tied him. Chico had Ben's Peacemaker. He balanced it in his strong hand, grunting with laconic admiration. Squatting, he unbuckled Ben's cartridge belt and was straightening as the Wells Fargo man started to regain consciousness. Chico kicked Ben in the ribs as he draped the cartridge belt across his shoulder. He tucked Ben's Colt into his waistband.

Toreno walked to the door. Turning his head, he could look across an expanse of comparatively open ground to the dark hills a few miles from town. He squatted on his heels, dragging his fingers through the warm dirt. "We will wait, Chico," he said patiently.

Behind them, cheek pressing into the dirty straw floor, Ben Craig also waited. There was a goose-egg lump behind his left ear and a sharp throbbing between his eyes. The two thick shadows in the doorway were somewhat blurred by the pounding pain in his head. But he heard Toreno's quiet voice calling the man beside him Chico.

Chico Montero!

Even in the bad light of the stable yard Ben recognized the figure squatting beside Toreno. It was the dull-faced Yaqui peon who had ridden on the seat of the stage from Saludad!

CHAPTER THIRTEEN

— Riders in the Night —

From farther down the street Sam Jelco had listened to the fight in The Hangout. He had waited patiently until he saw Ben Craig emerge and lose himself in the shadows beyond. The piebald horse he and Ben had trailed to Padre Valley was at the rail, bait for whoever was interested. Sam grinned coldly. He had ridden by The Hangout earlier, and the horse had not been there. Now it was in plain view, just shouting to be spotted.

It had hooked Ben Craig . . . but whoever had planted the animal there had underestimated the Wells Fargo agent. Sam didn't. Ben must have found out what he was after, and he was headed there now. Sam shrewdly guessed that the information was merely leading Ben back to Toreno.

About to start toward The Hangout, he pulled back into concealing shadows again as he saw the thick-bodied Yaqui peon move silently across the street and fade into darkness after Ben. Sam frowned. This wasn't the Sonora Kid.

But the man was evidently after Ben, and for no good reason.

Sam waited before deciding on his next move. And while he waited he saw Sheriff Rankin come up and go into the saloon. Curious, Sam crossed to the building and stepped up to one of the shattered windows. He listened quietly to the conversation inside, at first frowning, then smiling broadly.

So the sheriff thought Ben Craig was a gun-runner named Rick Stevens. And he was asking Stetson's help against Ben. It was like asking a wolf to protect his flock of sheep from the shepherd.

Sam pulled back into the shadows as Rankin came out. He watched the sheriff go to the tie-rack to mount Ben's buckskin. Then something caught Rankin's eye. He moved away, his face turned to the south.

Sam eased back and turned to look. He saw the signal fire, too, just before it burned out. Turning quickly, he saw Rankin cross back to the buckskin, mount and ride back to his office.

Some of the things he had heard since coming here began to make a pattern for Sam. Someone was running guns for Chico Montero, the revolutionary leader across the Border, but someone else had to pay for them first. And it could be that the Sonora Kid, with ninety thousand dollars in his saddlebags, was that man.

He started to follow Rankin, only to be brought up short by the shot that came close to killing the sheriff. He didn't see what happened to Rankin, but he caught a glimpse of Jesse Kane as the man rode past . . . riding Ben's buckskin horse!

Sam whirled and ran back to The Hangout hitchrack. The piebald was still there, mean and rangy; a much better animal than the Indian pony he had ridden into Padre Valley.

He was untying the animal when Lute sauntered out of the saloon. The outlaw stiffened as he spotted Sam. His voice bit coldly. "That's my horse, mister—"

Sam faced him; he was in a hurry. "Not any more," he said shortly. "I'm borrowin' him—"

He saw Lute go for his gun, and this was what he wanted. . . . Sam drew and killed the man before he cleared leather.

"Don't have time to bring you back to Abilene for the bounty on you, Lute," he growled. He swung up into the saddle of the piebald, whirled away from the rack. Stetson and his men were a little slow coming out to investigate. . . . They saw Lute lying facedown across the steps, heard the quick rhythm of the piebald's hoofs as Sam galloped away.

Stetson knelt slowly by Lute's body.

"Dead?" someone asked.

Stetson nodded. His face had a pinched bleakness. The Maverick's Hangout had suddenly become a very unhealthy place for his men!

Lying on his side, muscles testing the slack in the rope binding him, Ben did not see the signal fire. But he heard Toreno grunt and start to his feet.

"It is the sign," the stableman said. "*Andale*! We will hitch the wagon, Chico."

They stepped back inside the stable, stepping over Ben and moving into the darkness beyond. Shod hoofs thumped on the hard-packed earthen floor as a team was quickly harnessed. Toreno did not light up. He must have harnessed teams a hundred times under similar circumstances, for he was ready in a remarkably short time.

"Get him into the wagon," Toreno ordered his brother.

The Mexican chieftain bent over the Wells Fargo man, made a quick survey of the bonds around Ben's wrists, his legs. Satisfied, he heaved Ben up to his muscle-padded shoulder and walked out into the yard. He handled Ben's one hundred and eighty pounds with little effort.

An old spring wagon lay backed up against the adobe stable wall, half hidden by its shadow. Chico dumped Ben over the tailgate and turned to help Toreno back the harnessed team into place between the wagon tongue.

Toreno took a quick look at Ben lying on his back in the wagon bed. "*Por Dios*!" he muttered under his breath. He climbed heavily into the wagon, pulled out a handkerchief from his pants pocket and stuffed it between Ben's teeth, tying another around Ben's face to keep the gag in place.

Chico was already on the seat, waiting for him. Toreno frowned. "*Un momento*." He headed back into the stable and came out with a horse blanket which he threw over Ben.

The wagon tilted and creaked as Toreno climbed into the seat and gathered up the reins. They drove to the gate in the corral and Chico jumped down and opened it. The wagon rolled out, turning up the dark alley.

Lying on the hard wagon bed, Ben felt a grim helplessness seize him. He had no idea where Chico and Toreno were going. But he had no doubt as to what would happen to him when they got there.

A savage fury roiled through him. Never the kind of man to give up, he began to squirm along the wagon bed, seeking something, anything, that might offer him a chance of getting free.

The blanket that covered him smelled of stale horse sweat. He twisted and rolled over, bringing the blanket with him. When he rolled back the blanket was under him and he could look up and see the stars. The cool night air felt good in his lungs.

He was lying on his back, almost under the seat. Chico turned, his broad face looming over Ben, his black eyes studying the trussed man. Then Chico turned away.

The weight of his body on his bound hands was painful, and Ben twisted slowly, trying to bring his arms away from under him. Something sharp cut a gash across the back of his right hand. Ben froze, hope causing a sudden pounding to sound in his ears.

Slowly, carefully, he probed around with his fingers. A piece of strap iron, laid as reinforcement across the wagon bed, had obviously worn thin with the years. It had broken through, and a section of it was raised sufficiently to provide a ragged but effective cutting edge.

Ben's jaws clamped on the gag in his mouth. If this trip lasted long enough, the two men on the seat might yet run into a devil of a surprise!

The wagon jolted along fairly level country; then it began to climb. Ben could tell it was climbing by the tilting of the wagon bed and the increasingly labored breathing of the horses pulling it.

Ben's arms were growing numb. His shoulders ached. He could feel the blood trickle warm and sticky between his fingers from the several small gashes in his wrists. But with every passing moment now he knew he was freeing himself.

The two men riding above him had not spoken since they had climbed into the seat. It was Chico who broke the silence. He said in a low, harsh voice: "Someone is behind us, Toreno. I hear him . . . riding!"

Ben Craig tensed. Craning his neck, he could see Chico's broad frame limned against the stars above him. The man was turning, peering back along the rough mountain road.

Ben put all the strength remaining in his powerful shoulders against his frayed bonds. He felt them loosen. He saw Chico drop his gaze to him. There was a frowning regard in the peon's eyes.

Toreno's whisper reached Ben. "Wait, Chico! I'll see who it is!"

Chico's gaze lifted again to the road where a horse's shod hoofs rang clearly in the night.

Ben worked swiftly, savagely. His hands were still imprisoned. He doubled his wrists, curling his fingers inward to pluck at the loosening rope.

The rider coming up the road behind them approached at a suddenly wary jog. Toreno's whisper was barely audible. "It is the sheriff, Chico."

Ben's hands were free now. But his legs were still tied and he couldn't risk tearing the gag from his mouth to warn Rankin. Chico loomed above him, alert and deadly, and any suspicious motion from Ben would bring Chico's attention to him.

Rankin's voice came clearly through the stillness, cold and suspicious. "What are you doing out here, Toreno?"

The fat Mexican's voice held the proper note of surprise and relief. "Oh, it is you, Sheriff Rankin! I am driving my cousin, Pancho, to see our uncle Tomas who lives on the other side of the Santa Maria. Pancho has not visited with Uncle Tomas in many years—"

Rankin was drawing near the wagon. Ben heard the faint scrape of metal against leather and guessed that Chico now had a gun in his hand. Ben began to draw his legs under him for a desperate move. . . .

"See another rider come this way? Riding a big buckskin horse?"

Toreno shook his head. "No other rider, *Senor* Rankin."

Rankin was almost up to the wagon now. He straightened in his stirrups, his voice suddenly sharpening. "Hey! Whom do you have in the wagon?"

Ben rolled over just as Chico Montero fired. He glimpsed the flash of the gun over his head. He lurched up to his knees and caught hold of Montero's gun arm, extended over him. He jerked the man off the seat, down into the wagon, and managed to hook his left arm around Chico's throat as the squat Yaqui peon fell.

Ben's right hand was clamped on Montero's gun wrist. His bound legs hampered him, but he had the advantage of a stanglehold around the Mexican's neck. Montero threshed wildly, trying to shake Ben's arm from around his neck. Failing, he jammed his gun hand under him, hoping the muzzle was against Ben's body as he pulled trigger.

The shot was muffled by their bodies. Ben felt the flash burn of powder against his side. Montero arched his back in a sudden spasm as the bullet tore into him; a sigh gusted out of him as he went limp.

Toreno's shotgun blasted heavily a split-second behind the report of a Colt from behind the wagon. The wagon tilted as the frightened horses wheeled wildly. Toreno's bitter cursing was short-lived as he was hurled from the seat.

Ben shoved Montero's body aside and came up in an awkward crouch, tearing the gag from his mouth. He had a moment in which to notice that Toreno was no longer in the seat; then the stampeding team, lunging wildly, upset him. Ben fell back across Montero's body.

The horses were running without direction now. The wagon lurched as Ben tried to roll over and regain his footing. He slid across the bed, jamming hard against the wagon side.

Ben's teeth locked. He had to get off the wagon before it overturned or smashed against some obstruction. The wagon lurched again, bounced erratically, and Ben knew the team had left the mountain road. The Wells Fargo man gripped the wagon side and steadied himself. The team was headed for a clump of jack pine. The frightened animals swerved sharply at the last moment, and Ben vaulted over the wagon side as he felt it tip away from him.

He landed on his feet and immediately lost his balance, rolling downslope in a small slide of rocks and earth. He heard the wagon come apart, then a horse screamed in sharp, chilling pain.

Ben quickly freed his legs. The noise had died out on the dark hills. In the night the jack pine clump loomed as a thick solid blackness. A horse moved away from it, its harness making a small metallic sound.

Ben climbed back up the slope to what was left of the wagon. He found his Colt beside a broken wheel. His cartridge belt was still draped around Montero's shoulder.

Ben took a long breath. He had been lucky tonight. He felt tired and bruised as he cinched his belt around his waist and reloaded the gun. It felt good in his holster.

It took Ben Craig twenty minutes to backtrack his way to where Sheriff Rankin had caught up with the wagon. He half expected to find Toreno's body lying on the road, but the winding mountain passage was empty until he rounded a bend and saw a bay horse standing in the shadows just off the trail.

Ben's quick, searching glance picked up Rankin's shadowy figure. The sheriff was propped against a boulder off the trail, sitting with his long legs spread out in front of him. The bay's reins were looped around his left arm—and he was holding a Colt in his lap.

He seemed to be asleep . . . or dead. His head hung down on his chest.

Ben paced up to him. Rankin stirred, as if the sound of Ben's approach had awakened him. Or had he been waiting?

His gun lifted and targeted Ben, and Ben lunged aside a split-second before the muzzle blasted a bullet at him. The Colt kicked sharply out of Rankin's fingers and he tried to grab it, a small groan escaping from his tight lips.

Ben stepped in fast and kicked the gun out of Rankin's reach.

Rankin's face was pinched; he was hurt and he showed it. His eyes had the wet shine of pain in them.

Ben hunkered down beside the man, not quite sure where Rankin fitted in the picture but unwilling to see him bleed to death. He could see that Rankin's coat was darkening as blood spread its stain through it.

"How badly are you hurt?" he asked coldly.

Rankin moved bloodless lips. "I'll live—to see you hang!"

Ben grinned sourly. "That's tough talk for a Harvard man." He opened Rankin's coat and examined the bullet hole in the sheriff's upper shoulder. "You've got more luck than you deserve," he added cheerfully. "If we can stop you from bleeding to death, you'll live."

He worked swiftly, using Rankin's clean white handkerchief wadded thickly to stop the blood oozing from the bullet hole, tying it in place with bandages stripped from the sheriff's white shirt.

Rankin remained silent until Ben finished. Then, puzzled, he asked: "What are you after, Stevens?"

"I'm not Stevens." Ben's voice was curt. He turned his head and glanced into the shadows where the road curved out of sight. "Where's Toreno?"

Rankin shook his head; he didn't know.

Ben turned to him. "Look, my name's Ben Craig. Wells Fargo special agent." He saw a sneer of disbelief start across Rankin's pain-pinched mouth, and he reached for his wallet, holding his credentials for the other to see.

Rankin's eyes rounded. "Kane," he whispered

harshly. "Kane told me—" He choked back his bitter anger.

Ben frowned. "I don't know what your deputy told you, Sheriff, but I came to Padre Valley on the trail of the Sonora Kid. I want the Kid and the money he stole from that Wells Fargo express box."

Rankin nodded in bitter understanding. "Ninety thousand dollars! More than enough to pay for Chico Montero's guns!" He ran his tongue across his dry lips. "Reckon I've been a fool, Ben. I've got a commission as a deputy United States marshal. I was sent down here because we received a tipoff that a gun-runner named Rick Stevens had arranged to supply Chico with a thousand rifles. That's all I had to go on. I'd never seen Rick Stevens before, and I didn't know who was going to put up the money for those guns—"

"The Sonora Kid!" Ben's voice was harsh. "That's why the Kid held up the east-bound express: to get money for those guns!"

Rankin nodded. "I waited for Rick to come into the valley, Ben. This morning, when you showed up, Jesse Kane said you were Rick Stevens." His voice was bitter. "He fooled me completely. All the while I waited for Stevens to show up, he was in my office, waiting for the man who was going to buy his guns to get in touch with him."

"Jesse Kane?"

Rankin lifted his head and gestured to the road. "It must be Kane. He tried to kill me tonight. He took your horse and came this way. I know that now. I thought it was you. I believed him when he told me you were Stevens, even after I saw the signal fire on Santa Maria Hill."

Ben turned to look up the dark mountain. "Then he's up there somewhere. That's where Toreno was going, too: to a rendezvous with the Sonora Kid."

He swung back to Rankin. "I'll get you into the saddle. You think you can hang on long enough to make it back to town?"

Rankin grinned weakly. "Long enough to try to get help for you, Ben."

He forced himself to sit straight after Ben got him aboard his bay horse. He looked down on the tall man he had wanted to kill.

"Ben!" he whispered. "I don't care about Kane. But when you get the Sonora Kid . . ." He paused, his lips twisting with a touch of sadness. "Make it easy for her . . . when you tell her, later. . . ."

Ben looked closely at him, not quite following Rankin's thought. But the sheriff was turning the bay, heading down the mountain road toward the lights of Avalon in the distance.

CHAPTER FOURTEEN

— The Sonora Kid —

Carlos Cambriano, alias the Sonora Kid, paced impatiently up and down the narrow footpath in front of the shrine of Saint Mary. The life-size wooden saint under the small thatch-roofed shelter eyed him with silent sympathy. Over the long years the sinners had been many who had visited this shrine, kneeling for a moment to ask forgiveness.

But Carlos was not asking for forgiveness.

He finished his fourth cigaret and reached nervous fingers into the pocket of his snug-fitting charro jacket for another. What was holding Stevens up? He had made all the arrangements long ago, even before the holdup of the train outside of Boxwood City. He had heard of Rick Stevens, a man who would supply any number of guns—at a price. Rick had named his price, and Carlos had agreed to it.

Even the signal that was to alert Stevens that Carlos was ready to make payment—that had been arranged. All through an intermediary—through a grapevine arrangement that ran from Carlos to Toreno to the intermediary to Stevens.

The Sonora Kid stopped by the shrine to scrape a match on the side of the shelter. His face was dark and nervous in the match flare.

Stevens had never seen him—nor had he met the gun-runner. But only Stevens would know what the fire he had lighted meant. Stevens—and Toreno. Good old faithful Toreno!

From where he waited the Kid could look down into the blackness of Padre Valley—to the patchwork of small lights that made up Avalon. Somewhere between the town and the hill a man was riding to meet him.

The guns! All Carlos wanted were the guns Stevens had promised. He smiled grimly. All his life, it now seemed, had been pointed to this moment, to the day when he would arm a thousand men and watch them wreak their vengeance on the "gringos" who had taken over the land which rightfully belonged to his people.

He let his thoughts drift ahead to the meeting with Chico Montero. He had never met the revolutionary leader, but Toreno had told him of the man; painted a picture of a zealous patriot, a sort of Robin Hood of old Mexico. He saw himself at the head of the wagon caravan loaded with the modern rifles he had bought from Stevens, riding into Montero's mountain camp and being received by the great patriot. . . .

The soft snorting of a horse pulled him back to the present. The Kid whirled, a hand quick on his Colt as he peered back into the shadows from which he had come.

Had someone followed him? He had waited until his father had retired, and he had made sure Julia was in her room before leaving the hacienda. In case anyone inquired of him, he had left word with Juan that he was on his way back to town to see a college friend of his who had just arrived.

He waited now, a shadow against the blackness of the shrine enclosure—a slim and deadly figure who had learned long ago that his hand was quick and his eye good and that any man, big or small, could be killed by a bullet.

For three years now he had played a game with death. The slim patrician son of respected Jose Cambriano who went to study at the University of Mexico City was a world apart from the deadly killer who raided north of the Border as the Sonora Kid.

At first it had been his way of showing defiance, the course his rebellion had taken. In the deadly game of gunplay in which the hard-eyed men north of the Border seemed to excel, he, Carlos Cambriano, held his own! It had given him a peculiar exultation, and it fed his burning pride to plan and execute the raids that became the trademark of the Sonora Kid.

It had not been for money that he had robbed and killed, although he had always taken money. The son of Don Jose did not need money. He had given it away, the stolen money, dribbling it out through the fingers of Jacinto, the owner of the *Corrida de Toros* cafe, from which, he was assured, the money found its way into needy Mexican hands.

And then Toreno had pointed out that Chico Montero had a thousand men in the hills less than twenty miles away. A thousand men with a thousand American rifles—?

The sound of a walking horse, from down-trail this time, pulled his attention away from the darkness beyond the shrine.

The night was heavy with waiting. The Kid crouched like a hunting animal, his hand tight on his gun butt. It had to be Rick Stevens! Ben Craig had eluded the trap set for him in the garden behind the *Corrida* . . . but Toreno had assured him that the Wells Fargo agent would be dead before the night was over.

The walking horse stopped. In the deep silence Carlos could hear his own nervous breathing and silently cursed the rider in the shadows. What was Rick Stevens afraid of?

The voice reached up out of the down-slope darkness. "Hold it, Kid. I'm Stevens!"

Carlos let out a slow breath. He straightened and moved away from the shadows by the shrine, pausing on the edge of starlight illuminating the footpath. "Come ahead!" he called out. "I'm the Sonora Kid!"

Some faint sound, almost like a sharp intake of breath, drifted to him from the quiet above the shrine. Or was it off to the left? He turned, listened intently, frowning, uneasy. Was he so nervous he was now hearing things? He shrugged and turned back to the rider downslope, unseen, waiting. He cursed his ragged nerves. "Come up where I can see you, Stevens!" he snarled.

The rider came forward, moving slowly up into the starlit footpath. Carlos recognized the big buckskin horse first, and panic sledged him in the pit of his stomach. *Ben Craig!* For one terrible moment he was unable to move; then his hand jerked at the butt of his Colt. . . .

The rider's voice cracked like a too taut riata: *"Hold it!"*

Carlos' gun muzzle didn't clear his holster. Very slowly he let the gun slide back into place, his eyes narrowed and bitter on the thick-shouldered man riding the buckskin. It wasn't Ben! The man was Jesse Kane, Rankin's hardcase deputy!

Kane's Colt was levelled at Carlos' stomach, held capably enough in Kane's bandaged hand. "I heard you were fast, Kid," the deputy said coldly, "so I made sure!"

Carlos licked his dry lips. He had played his cards to get rid of Ben Craig, only to have his plans wrecked by this dumb deputy. How had Kane found out? Had he, too, been waiting for his signal?

Kane must have guessed what was going on in the Kid's mind. He laughed shortly. "Fooled you, too, eh, Kid?" He slid his Colt back into the holster. "Don't let the badge bother you. I'm Rick Stevens—the man with the rifles!"

Carlos stiffened. "You're a liar!" he said grimly.

"And you're a fool!" Stevens snapped testily. His face was slightly lopsided from the swelling around his mouth. "I've got a thousand rifles, late model Winchesters. A hundred and fifty rounds for every rifle, and two field pieces. That's what you wanted, wasn't it?" Kane's lips, swollen to almost twice their usual size, twisted grotesquely. "That's what you ordered . . . for Chico Montero!"

The suspicion in Carlos died hard. "I don't know what you're talking about," he said stiffly.

Kane swore. "Look, Kid, I'm in a hurry. Now quit stalling around. I don't usually go around advertising myself," he added harshly. "In my business I've got to be careful. I had an idea the authorities would get wind of this deal. I was right. I came to Padre Valley ahead of time, and I spotted the deputy marshal right off."

Carlos shook his head, not quite following the man.

"Listen, Kid!" Kane's voice was impatient. "Arch Rankin's a deputy United States marshal. I knew him the day I rode into Avalon. He didn't know me. But he was down here because of me and you . . . because someone back in Austin got wind of our deal." He grinned bleakly. "The thought of a bunch of armed *revolucionistas* camped on the Border must have shaken the authorities as far away as Washington." He laughed shortly. "So I moved in on Rankin. He was waiting for Stevens to show up and tip his hand, and there I was, at his right hand. I was waiting, too, Kid; waiting for some joker to show up who I could convince Rankin was Rick Stevens."

Carlos nodded, breathing easier now. "You sure fooled me," he admitted.

Rick Stevens, alias Jesse Kane, chuckled. "I got my man this afternoon. The tall man who owned this horse I'm riding." He frowned, eyeing the Kid with slight puzzlement. "I didn't know he was a friend of yours."

It was Carlos' turn to laugh—a short, bitter sound. "Sometimes a man can get too smart," he muttered. "The rider you tangled with in the plaza is Ben Craig, a Wells Fargo agent!"

Stevens leaned over the buckskin's arched neck, his eyes boring into the Kid. "You lying to me, Kid?"

Carlos sneered. “I nearly killed a piebald horse trying to outrun that horse you’re on, and the man who followed me from Boxwood City was Ben Craig!”

Stevens swore. “You knew that when you shot a gun out of my hand?”

Carlos nodded grimly. “I saw a chance to throw him off my trail—for a while, anyway. He didn’t know me. It would take some time before he’d begin to suspect the man who had saved his life!”

Stevens wiped his lips with his sleeve. “Well, Wells Fargo agent or not, he ain’t gonna bother us now, Kid. Just before I left I saw him head for The Maverick’s Hangout. There was a piebald at The Hangout rail—”

Carlos’ voice broke in, choked, and harsh. “That fool, Toreno!”

“Maybe not too much of a fool.” Stevens chuckled. “If he left that piebald there as bait, it worked.” He made a gesture down-slope. “That Maverick bunch are no pushovers. Ben walked into that place, and even from the sheriff’s office it sounded like one devil of a fight! Rankin ran out to investigate. I hung back, waiting for your fire. About five minutes later Rankin came back, riding this buckskin. So I got rid of Rankin, borrowed this cayuse, and rode up here to meet with you. Way I figger it, Kid, Ben Craig walked into a little more than he could handle in The Hangout!"

Carlos breathed a sigh of relief. "So both Rankin and Ben Craig are dead?" He spat out the soggy butt which had gone dead in his mouth. "All right, Stevens, it's a deal. You have the guns?"

The shot made a sharp, echoing report in the night, the echoes bouncing from the slopes. Stevens, about to reply, twisted in the saddle. "What was that—?"

Another gunshot punched through the mountain stillness, followed almost immediately by the heavy blasting sound of a shotgun! Then silence closed in around the reports, sopping up the sounds.

In the stillness another sound identified itself to the two waiting men—the sound of a wagon being pulled by two running horses. They both waited tensely, sensing what was building up in the darkness below them; waited with sucked-in breaths for the crash that seemed inevitable. It came, finally, a faint crashing noise that rattled among the hills for a few seconds before it died out.

Behind Carlos, and from above the shrine, a horse snorted in fright and minced into view, fighting the bit between its teeth. The Kid whirled sharply, his Colt snaking out; the shock of recognition turned his muzzle at the last split-second.

The roan mare reared up with a wild scream as Carlos' gun flared almost in its face. Julia lost her balance. She fell backward, landing heavily on her side. The fall momentarily stunned her.

Carlos ran to his sister and crouched over her. His face was white, his knuckles knobbing as he held his gun. Stevens was fighting the buckskin, trying to keep himself in the saddle.

Carlos looked down at Julia as she groaned softly. How much had she heard? The thought beat wildly in his head. How much did Julia know?

Stevens finally gained control of the animal and spurred him up close. "Where'd she come from?" he demanded thickly.

Carlos made a gesture up the path. "I left her in her room. She must have followed me." His lips twisted bitterly. "Must have been listening to us—"

Stevens cut him off. "She's yore problem, Kid!" he growled. "Let's get out of here! Where's the money?"

Carlos was staring at his sister. She stirred, tried to sit up. He made no move to help her.

Stevens licked his lips impatiently. "Where's the money?" he repeated harshly.

Carlos glanced up at him. "Where are the guns?" he countered grimly.

"Cached in the valley." Stevens glanced nervously into the down-slope darkness. "I'll lead you to them as soon as you hand over the money."

Julia sat up. Her pained eyes looked into those of her brother. Carlos turned his head away, straightened. "I don't have the money here," he said to Stevens. "You'll have to ride back to town with me."

Stevens exploded. "You stalling me, Kid?"

Carlos shook his head. "I've got the money, but not with me—"

Stevens jerked a thumb behind him. "You heard those shots, that wagon! Something's gone wrong down there!" He leaned forward in the saddle, his eyes dangerous. "We won't have time to try and outguess each other. If you're trying to hold out on me now—?"

Carlos shook his head. "You'll get the money . . . after you show me where the guns are hidden!"

He turned back to Julia as she said: "Carlos." Her voice was low, hurt. "The Sonora Kid. The man who dynamited a train just to get money. Money he didn't need—"

Carlos stiffened. "Now you know, Julia," he said harshly.

Julia shook her head. "I don't know. . . . Why?" Her eyes searched his face. "Why?"

Stevens cut in, quick and deadly: "You tell her why later, after I've got the money, Kid!"

Carlos turned to look at him; he sucked

in a harsh breath. "I can't let her stay here, and I can't take her with me—"

"Kid, I want the money!" Stevens snarled. "I don't care what you do about her—"

They both turned quickly as someone down the path chuckled coarsely. "Wal, wal, boys . . . arguin' over money?"

Carlos made an instinctive motion to his gun and froze. . . . Stevens, a vulnerable target on the buckskin, didn't even try. They eyed the big man who moved toward him.

Sam Jelco stopped a few feet away. The gun in his hand gave him command of the situation; he was very pleased with himself. He looked at Carlos.

"I'll take her off yore hands, Kid," he said, "for ninety thousand dollars!"

Carlos stared at him. Stevens said harshly: "Who are you?"

Sam grinned. "The Kid oughta know. I trailed him all the way down from that train he held up, outside Boxwood City." As Carlos showed no sign of recognition: "Name's Sam Jelco." He seemed grieved at their lack of recognition.

"The bounty hunter?" Stevens rasped.

Sam nodded, pleased. He looked at Carlos. "I started out for ten thousand dollars . . . what you're worth up north, preferably dead." He turned his gaze to Julia, who was staring at him in horror. "But I've just changed my mind. I'll do you a favor and take her with me. Ninety thousand dollars should set us both up nicely, down in Vera Cruz."

Carlos shook his head. "That money is for guns—"

Sam thumbed back the hammer of his Colt. "Guns, Kid?" His grin was cold. "They mean more to you than yore sister?"

Carlos said desperately: "I'll double the ten-thousand-dollar reward—"

He cut off as Sam shifted the deadly muzzle to Stevens. "Reckon I'll just get rid of him, Kid. Then you won't have to worry about no guns!"

Stevens was stiff in the saddle. His words came slowly, bitterly. "Give him the money, Kid!"

Sam smiled at Carlos. "See?" he chuckled. "No problem—"

The shotgun charge smashed into his broad back, killing him instantly. He was knocked forward on his face, dying at Carlos' feet!

CHAPTER FIFTEEN

— Death on Santa Maria Hill —

Toreno stalked into view, slipping a fresh shell into his shotgun. He barely glanced at Sam's body. His eyes slipped from Carlos and Julia to Stevens . . . the muzzle of the shotgun tilted up at him.

"The guns!" he said harshly.

Stevens looked at Carlos and nodded. "I will show you. But first the money."

Toreno cut him off. "The guns first!" he said thickly. "We will talk of pay later!"

Stevens balked. He could read what was in Toreno's mind; his payment would be a buckshot charge, like the one Sam Jelco had received.

He turned to Carlos. "It was a deal, Carlos . . . a gentleman's agreement. Fifty thousand dollars for the guns—"

Carlos nodded. "I'll take care of things, Toreno," he said brusquely. "Stay with Julia. I'll ride down into the valley with him, pay him off . . ."

"You'll shut up!" Toreno snapped. His voice was short, ugly. He had just seen his brother die, the work of years of scheming jeopardized.

He was in no mood to continue his game with Carlos.

Carlos reacted with stunned surprise. "Toreno!"

"Chico Montero is dead!" Toreno snapped. "Now I want the guns . . . to avenge him!" He swung back to Stevens. "You will take me to them . . . *now!*"

Carlos stepped forward to intervene. He was still shocked by the news of Montero's death, angered by Toreno's tone.

"I promised him payment," he said sharply. "A gentleman's agreement, Toreno!"

Toreno sneered. "Gentleman?" He spat on the ground. "Fool is the better word, Carlos." As Carlos recoiled from him: "The guns are all my brother and I wanted . . . guns enough to put us in power. The money would come later, Carlos . . . later!"

Carlos stood still for a moment, feeling Julia's eyes on him, burning with the shame of his betrayal, of his use by this man whose patriotism was a mockery. Then he took a step forward, his hands reaching out for Toreno. . . .

From the darkness behind Toreno Ben's voice whipped coldly: "Toreno!"

Toreno whirled with the shotgun, and Ben fired, his bullets tearing into Toreno's stomach, spinning him around. Toreno's shotgun blasted heavily as he fell, the charge smashing Carlos back, his right arm and shoulder riddled!

Julia screamed!

Stevens drew and fired once at Ben as the Wells Fargo agent came toward him. The shot seemed to trigger a spring in the buckskin under him . . . the animal sunfished him out of the saddle. Stevens landed sprawling, his Colt jarred out of his hand. He made a rolling lunge for the gun just as the buckskin horse kicked out with both hind legs. The animal's right hind hoof laid open the gun-runner's scalp from above his left eye midway to the back of his head.

Ben shifted his attention to the girl. Julia was in the buckskin's path, and the frightened animal was lunging with bared teeth at her. The horse had been badly roweled by Stevens, and at the moment all strangers were enemies to be slashed and pounded beneath his deadly hoofs!

Ben's left hand shot up to the dangling bit reins as the buckskin reared high over the girl. "Hold it, boy—hold it!" Ben's arm yanked the buckskin aside. "It's me! You remember me!"

The buckskin quieted as Ben caressed the stallion's arched neck. "It's all right, boy," Ben said softly. His eyes narrowed at the blood oozing from the horse's spur-ripped flanks. "No wonder you acted up!"

From the darkness up-slope a horse snorted. Hoofs drummed in the quiet, fading down-slope. . . .

Ben spun around, his eyes searching for the man he knew as the Sonora Kid. Julia's brother, Carlos!

Julia's voice was a sob. "He's gone, Ben!"

Ben turned to her. Julia had started to run after her brother as Ben quieted the buckskin. Now she turned to look back at the Wells Fargo man, her mouth trembling. "He's badly hurt . . . he's dying. . . ."

Ben took a deep breath. "I'll do what I can for him, Julia." He turned to step up into the buckskin's saddle, but the girl ran back; she held him in check. "Ben, let him go!"

Ben took her wrists in his hands. To him the man escaping in the darkness was the Sonora Kid—a killer he had tracked seven hundred miles. To the girl the man was her brother. And in that moment Julia Cambriano was thinking only of that.

"I can't!" Ben said.

He did not want to hurt this girl who had been hurt enough that day—but he couldn't turn away now.

The girl buried her face in his shirt. Ben felt her whole body quiver, but she did not cry aloud. He held her for a silent moment, feeling her softness and her nearness and briefly affected by it. Then a wry smile crinkled his lips.

He pushed her away slowly. "Arch Rankin is a lucky man," he said gently. Then he stepped up into the buckskin's saddle. "Your horse is waiting, Julia. Go on home. There's nothing more you can do here."

He whirled his horse around, not waiting for her reply.

Julia watched his horse fade into the down-trail darkness. In the mountain quiet the sound of hoofs seemed to pound for a long time, matching the pounding in her heart. Then other sounds turned her about. Riders! From the hacienda!

She watched Juan and a half-dozen of her father's vaqueros loom up out of the night, riding armed and grim-faced. Juan's mouth tightened as he saw Julia. His gaze went past her to the bodies on the footpath behind her.

He dismounted and went to her. Julia said simply: "Take me home, Juan."

The old Mexican nodded. "The shots in the hills bothered your father's sleep," he said. "When he found out you and Carlos were gone—" He shrugged, turning to stare again at the bodies by the shrine. Even as he looked Stevens stirred and began to paw at his bloody face.

Juan made a motion to the riders at his back. "Take them all back to the hacienda," he ordered. Turning to Julia, softly: "Don Jose is waiting for you."

CHAPTER SIXTEEN

— The Last Payment —

Much of Avalon still adhered to the old patterns of living, and thus most of its citizens were asleep when Sheriff Rankin, drooped wearily over the neck of his horse, rode past the first scattered buildings. He had kept his bay to a steady pace, letting it take its own way back to town and concentrating on fighting the throbbing pain in his shoulder.

Between spasms random thoughts had flitted through his head, and as he neared town a feeling of shame and resentment grew in him. He had fancied himself a knowing and capable federal officer, and yet he had let Stevens trick him, make a fool of him. Even more: because of Stevens he had made a deal with Cal Stetson, boss of the Maverick gang. This last rankled deeply in his bitter thoughts.

He knew now that Stetson must have known that the man he had called Stevens was Ben Craig, a Wells Fargo agent. Rankin remembered how Stetson had agreed too readily to his terms—much too readily!"

He had, in fact, given Stetson and his men

carte blanche to kill the special agent. Stetson, who was behind most of the trouble in Padre Valley—the man he had deliberately ignored because of the bigger threat posed by Chico Montero.

It might have been the giddiness in Rankin's head, or a hard core of stubbornness that nagged at him to straighten out this last affair. By rights he should have headed directly for Doctor Alvarez's house . . . or at least have searched out Pablo and enlisted his help. Instead he turned on San Pablo Avenue and rode past the darkened buildings.

The Maverick's Hangout had a reputation for never closing. It was living up to it. The splash of light from its kerosene lamps still placed at each end of the bar seeped out to the street in front of Rankin. He reached for his Colt, then paused as behind him, coming up fast, he heard a running horse! Rankin swiveled in his saddle. He saw nothing, but the sound of hoofbeats grew louder.

Ben Craig, he thought . . . and the lightness in his head was like wine, making him slightly giddy. He slid out of the saddle and hung weakly by the animal's side, his glance going back to The Hangout door where a burly man had stepped out to look down the street, drawn by the sound of the approaching rider.

Rankin shoved away from his horse and

started for the man in the saloon doorway. He had his Colt in his hand, down by his side. He called out to the man, his voice bleak: "This way, Sneed!"

Sneed turned and made a wild grab for his gun. Rankin's Colt came up, bucked in his hand. Sneed fell back against the batwings just as the rider loomed up out of the darkness.

Rankin was in the middle of the street, turning unsteadily, when the piebald brushed him. The animal's heavy shoulder spun him around like a rag doll. He fell forward on his hands and knees, still clutching his Colt—and surprise was like a chunk of ice shoved down his spine.

Carlos! It was Carlos, hanging like a burr over the piebald's neck, who had come by!

He heard The Hangout batwings slam violently as men piled out onto the small porch. In the distance he seemed to hear the echo of Carlos' horse—they sounded louder, instead of diminishing. Was the Kid coming back?

Stetson was the first man he saw as Rankin scrambled to his feet. The outlaw boss was staring up the street. . . . The men bunched around him scattered as Stetson made a sudden move for his shoulder gun.

The buckskin coming up behind Rankin didn't even break stride. Ben lifted himself in his stirrups, his Colt cutting down at the men in front of The Hangout.

Cal Stetson was spun around and slammed against the building by the slugs. The three men with him fired several wild shots, then dove back into the comparative safety of the saloon.

Ben reined in quickly by Rankin's side. A bullet slammed through the batwings, brushing his hat as he slid out of the saddle. The Wells Fargo agent emptied his gun into the saloon, aiming through the window at the lights he could see on the bar.

One of them went out in a spatter of oil. Then Ben grabbed Rankin's left arm and turned him to the buckskin. "Let's get out of here, Sheriff!"

No shots came from the saloon as Rankin was pulled up into the saddle behind Ben. But a bluish glow was flickering in the darkness behind the shattered windows; a glow that suddenly took on an ominous glare of yellow. . . .

Rankin leaned against Ben's back. "Carlos rode by, just before you showed up, Ben. He was headed for the plaza. . . ." His hand tightened on Ben's arm as the buckskin lunged away. "Probably find him in the *Corrida*. . . ."

But Carlos had not gone into the cantina. They found his piebald nosing the steps of the

Mission, reins dragging, flanks heaving from its long wild run. Ben swung out of saddle and glanced at the open doors of the church. Candlelight barely made an impression in the deep blackness of the interior.

Rankin wobbled up beside the special agent. "I'm coming with you," he said simply.

They followed gleaming spatters of blood up the worn stone steps, under the vaulted doorway. Ben took off his hat and sheathed his gun as he stepped inside.

His eyes probed the darkness. Several candles burned at the altar—others flickered eerily before the plaster saints in wall niches.

There was no movement, no sound, inside the church. Ben walked down the middle aisle, his sharp eyes picking out occasional blood splotches gleaming in the faint light. The blood trail led to a side door to the left of the altar rail.

A rotound, bald priest met them in this doorway. He had been expecting them, for he made the sign of the cross, then said: "This way," turning to the side exit.

They followed him along a shrub-bordered pathway to a small burial plot enclosed by a high spiked iron fence. The name Cambriano was lettered in iron over the small gate.

The Sonora Kid lay across an old grave of his ancestors. A small stone cross, gray and weathered by the years, lay overturned, revealing a hole dug under its foundation. Not a big hole; just big enough to hide the leather pouch holding ninety thousand dollars of Wells Fargo money.

Don Jose took his son's death hard. But he accepted it with pride, not questioning Ben's explanation that Carlos had been killed by Toreno while helping him in a fight with the gun-runners. The Wells Fargo agent saw no need to rub the salt of the truth into the bitter wound of the old man's grief.

Rick Stevens recovered from his scalp wound in Avalon's jail. The day he was well enough to ride with Ben out of Padre Valley, Ben Craig stopped by the Cambriano hacienda.

Arch Rankin was sitting on the veranda alongside Don Jose. Both men were now well enough to get about, but both enjoyed the attention they were receiving from the women of the house. Arch was in no hurry to leave.

He grinned as Ben dismounted and came up the steps. "I see you're ready to travel," he said. Stevens was sitting saddle on a dun horse, beside Ben's buckskin. His hands were manacled in front of him.

Ben nodded. "I'll turn him over to the authorities in Austin for you," he said. He turned to Don Jose. "Pablo's back in office. What's left of the Maverick bunch have quit the valley." He shrugged. "I have a feeling things will be quiet in Padre Valley from now on, Don Jose."

"Thanks to you and," he looked at Rankin, "my future son-in-law." He made a gesture of invitation to Ben. "My house and mine will always be open to you, *Senor* Craig."

Julia came out of the house, pausing by Rankin's chair. Her eyes still held a remote grief—and a gratefulness for Ben's lie. Rankin's hand closed over hers.

"Stay another ten days, Ben," he urged. "I need a good man at my wedding."

Ben reluctantly refused. "I've delayed too long," he murmured.

Julia came to him, raising her lips to him. "A best man's privilege, Ben," she said softly. He felt the warmth of her kiss briefly, and then she stepped back.

"Come back and visit us sometime, Ben."

Ben nodded. He turned and went down the steps and mounted his horse. The buckskin snorted softly as hc settled in the saddle.

The sun was hot on his back as he and Rick Stevens rode out of the yard, under the gate of the Cambrianos, and turned to the long road north . . . to Denver!